CHAPTER ONE

IT WAS reluctantly, as she stared out at the waters of the immense lake, that Jayme Warren was forced to acknowledge that she had set herself an impossible task. Yet it hadn't seemed at all impossible last night, she reflected unhappily. Though, last night, she'd had no idea just how vast Lake Garda was.

With her eyes on the shimmering expanse of unpolluted water she mused disconsolately on how last evening—after she had become acquainted with the fact that Tusco had moved to Torbole to windsurf—nothing had seemed simpler than that she should come to Torbole to find him.

Worriedly she strained her eyes into the distance, but, far from there being only one or two sailboard enthusiasts out there, as she had cosily supposed, there were literally a couple of hundred! Not only that, but—in addition to her being unable to make him out from any of the others windsurfing out there—with there being seemingly so many 'coming in' places, Tusco could beach his sailboard anywhere along the miles of shoreline when he had had sufficient sport for the day.

It was true that occasionally one of the brightly coloured wetsuited fraternity would tack on the strong breeze to the shore near her, but so far none of the few who had 'come in' anywhere in the direction of where she sat had been Tusco.

Glancing at her watch, Jayme saw that it was lunchtime, but she did not feel like eating—and she was glad about that. She had come to Italy on impulse and, of necessity, on a shoestring budget. The hour-long taxi ride to Torbole had been an unexpected expense which had sorely depleted her lire—but what else could she have done?

Her suitcase was down on the ground beside her as she pondered that last thought. Agreed, she could have asked about train services to Torbole, or made enquiries about a bus coming this way. But, since her Italian was next to non-existent, and with the frequency with which, so she was learning, Tusco changed his abode, it seemed to her that rather than save her money it was more important that she should get to Torbole quickly, before he moved on to somewhere else.

It puzzled her what he was doing hopping from one place to another all the time anyway, but no doubt he would tell her all about it when they met up again.

If they ever met up again, she thought glumly, as she sat on there, knowing that not until the last sailboard had gone from the lake would she move. Where would she go to anyway? She had no earthly idea where Tusco now lived.

Jayme sighed and stared at the transparent waters lapping the rocky shoreline in front of her. Fish, some of them quite large, swam where they would, but her attention soon strayed from them. In no time her thoughts were back to how last night, with dusk already having given way to nightfall, she had taken a taxi from the airport in Verona to the address which the man she loved, and who loved her, had given her on his return to Italy two months before.

Disappointment had awaited her, however, when, in answer to her, *'Permesso, parla inglese?'* and her subsequent enquiry for 'Signor Tusco Bianco?' she was informed, in better English than her phrasebook Italian, that Tusco had moved out some weeks before. While this explained why he had never answered one of her letters—because clearly he could not have received them—Jayme had felt more anxious than relieved.

As luck would have it, though, Tusco's ex-landlord was able to find his new address. And it was he, clearly liking the look of the trim platinum blonde with the sea-green eyes who stood on his doorstep, who called a taxi for her and told the taxi driver where to take her.

Disappointment awaited her again, though, when she rang the bell at an apartment some two miles distant. For when the door was opened it was not Tusco who stood there, but a solid and mature woman dressed all in black.

'*Permesso,*' Jayme went into her scant Italian again, 'but *parla inglese*?'

Clearly the woman did not, but without so much as a glimmer of a smile upon her ageing features she turned from Jayme and yelled back along the hall, in a voice that would shatter glass, 'Giorgio!'

The next thing Jayme knew was that a youth of about fifteen had come into the lighted hall and, after what sounded like an explosion of Italian between the two, the youth Giorgio was at the door too, asking politely. 'You are English, *signorina*?'

'Yes,' Jayme replied, experiencing a let-up of tension at being able to communicate. 'I'm...' she began, and was about to introduce herself as Tusco's fiancée when she hesitated. As yet, for all Tusco had asked her to marry him, they were not officially engaged. 'I'd like to see Signor Tusco Bianco—is he in?' she changed her mind to query of the waiting Giorgio.

At his reply, she promptly felt as though her heart had dropped to her boots.

'He does not live here no more,' Giorgio told her.

'He doesn't . . . ! He's left?' Jayme asked urgently, starting to feel quite desperate. But, calling up every scrap of backbone so as not to crumble, she quietly went on to question, 'Do you know where I might find him?'

Another explosion of Italian followed as Giorgio turned to the elderly lady. He then turned back to state, 'My grandmother, she say he has gone to Torbole to windsurf.'

'W. . .' Abruptly Jayme closed her mouth. She had been about to echo the word 'windsurf', but expressing her bafflement that Tusco had left the area where she had supposed him to be hard at work to spend some time windsurfing, of all things, was not going to be productive in her getting to him.

'Do you have his forwarding address?' she asked as she fought against a wave of near despair of ever seeing Tusco again, and waited while Giorgio repeated her question to his grandmother.

'No,' he quickly translated her answer. 'My grandmother thinks he is now living in Torbole.'

'Is Torbole far from here?' Jayme pushed tendrils of weariness away to enquire.

Giorgio had a quick discussion with his grandmother, then said, 'I think it's about seventy kilometres.'

Jayme's heart sank again. It was no good wishing that she had written to say she was coming. The sole reason that she was here was precisely because she *had* written, often, and because Tusco had not written at all, and she had been worried about him.

Feeling defeated, and suddenly very tired, she looked at Giorgio, who was listening intently to something his grandmother was telling him. Jayme guessed that they were waiting for her to go, so they could close the door, but since these people were a link with Tusco she felt she must question them some more before she thanked them politely and left.

Whether she was looking as weary as she felt, she had no idea, but as Giorgio's grandmother ended her quick stream of Italian, suddenly the woman looked directly at her, and, for the first time, offered a smile.

Then Giorgio was translating, 'My grandmother asks if you would wish to come inside and rest for a little.'

From somewhere Jayme found a smile too, and in next to no time she was comfortably ensconced in a homely sitting-room, and learning at first hand of the warmth and hospitality of the Italian people.

During the next half-hour she drank a welcome cup of coffee, was invited to call Giorgio by his first name, and his grandmother by the name of Signora Caselli. In turn, Jayme introduced herself and invited them both to use her first name, and smiled with the old lady, who made one syllable of her name and not the two that it was, when Giorgio insisted that she got it right.

'Jay—me, *Nonna*,' he instructed slowly.

'Jay—me,' his grandmother beamed as she obliged, clearly doting on her grandson.

Jayme still did not like to claim to be Tusco's fiancée—though she guessed that Signora Caselli had seen enough of the world to know that she was probably looking for him from some sort of romantic attachment, as she pursued the information she had so far given her.

'You said Torbole is about seventy kilometres from here—is it a very big place?' she enquired, and waited for the by now customary discussion which Giorgio had with his grandparent before he informed her.

'It is not so big. *Nonna* says it is one of the small towns on Lake Garda.'

Jayme had a feeling that Tusco had mentioned Lake Garda in the early days of their getting to know each other. But in any event, since water and windsurfing went hand in hand, so to speak, she did not feel any surprise at what Giorgio had just said. Though, as her hopes of finding Tusco dipped even further, it suddenly came to her that if this place Torbole was only a small town, then surely its lakeside area would be small too. And since Tusco had apparently moved to Torbole to do some windsurfing, what easier way of finding him was there than to present herself at the lakeside—and wait for him to appear?

'I must go to Torbole,' she murmured to Giorgio, and as he translated what she had said to his grandmother Jayme prepared to leave the friendly home, with just one more question on her lips. 'Can you tell me where I might find a taxi?'

Her question was translated back to Signora Caselli, and Jayme saw the disturbed look about the Italian woman. Within the next few minutes Giorgio had translated back that his grandmother was concerned that she could not have accommodation pre-booked in Torbole and that, as it was early September and still the tourist season, she might have some difficulty there. It was Signora Caselli's suggestion that she should take her guest-room for the night.

Jayme had to admit to feeling something akin to relief at the woman's kind offer. She was anxious to see Tusco as soon as she could, but she felt that a night's rest before she went on to Torbole might not be such a bad idea. She would pay for her night's lodgings, of course.

Surprisingly, she slept much better than she would have supposed, but she arose early and washed and dressed—with her thoughts on Tusco. She felt tremendously guilty when the uncomfortable niggle of doubt plagued her and she wondered what Tusco was doing seemingly taking a windsurfing holiday. The last time she had seen him, two months ago, besides vowing his undying love, he had vowed that he would labour night and day in order to earn and save sufficient funds to enable them to marry next year.

Jayme left the bathroom chiding herself that, while she was as keen as Tusco for them to be married next year, she did not want him labouring all hours so that that end could be achieved. Good heavens, she thought as she went to find Signora Caselli, Tusco had every right to some relaxation! He had probably been working like a Trojan ever since he had left England. He deserved to let up a bit.

'*Buon giorno,*' she smiled to Signora Caselli. Giorgio was not there that Tuesday morning—either gone home to his parents or to school, Jayme surmised, as she ate the breakfast which the *signora* had laid out for her.

Shortly afterwards, Jayme set about settling for her night's accommodation and trying to convey her grateful thanks to the elderly lady for taking her in last night.

When Signora Caselli beamed a smile and then, pointing to her watch, said, '*Tassi, nove,*' Jayme had reason to be grateful to her again. For, after she had stared at her blankly for a moment, it suddenly

dawned on her that her hostess must be saying that
a taxi had been booked for her.

'For nine?' Jayme queried, pointing to the figure
nine on her own watch.

'*Si,*' the lovely lady beamed...

Jayme's reverie was broken as just then a yellow,
black and fluorescent pink wetsuit-clad windsurfer
sailed to shore and beached his craft a little way away
from her. Hope flared briefly in her, but, as the young
man admiringly caught her glance, she could see that
he was not Tusco. Oh, where was he? Was he even in
Torbole?

She tried desperately hard not to feel totally defeated, but it was not easy. Apart from the worry of
wondering what on earth she would do if she didn't
see Tusco that day—as seemed to be growing more
and more likely—she had a job she had to get back
to as soon as she could. Her employer had been very
good about letting her have some time off, but he
would not be at all happy if she wasn't back at her
desk by the weekend. Also, her mother would be
waiting to hear that everything was all right. But how
could she ring and tell her that everything was all right,
when everything was so 'all wrong'?

The breeze was strong on the lake, but still the sun
was pleasantly warm as Jayme, in a pink and grey
checked cotton dress, dwelt for a while on thoughts
of her brave mother. Brave, she decided, was the only
word that fitted the way her mother had buckled to
when her husband had died six years before.

Jayme had been sixteen at the time and, shaken to
the core herself at losing her father, she had been of
an age to appreciate something of the utter, appalling
disaster it had been for her mother to lose the man
she had been so devoted to. That, unfortunately, had

not been the only disaster. A week after her dear husband's funeral, Audrey Warren, who had never had to concern herself with the household finances, had discovered that there would be no more money coming in. The pension scheme paid into by her late husband had some complicated clause which deemed that the sizeable monies due would not begin to be paid until fifty-five years from the date of Charles Warren's birth. Since Charles Warren had been barely forty-nine when he died, the pension due to his widow would be frozen for the next six years.

Perhaps from a need to talk and confide in someone, it was with Jayme, the eldest of her three daughters, that Audrey Warren shared what seemed at that time an insurmountable problem.

'What can we do?' Jayme asked, and decided on the spot. 'I'll leave school and get a job and...'

'No, Jayme, I don't want you to do that,' her mother had opposed that idea gently.

'But we have to have money from somewhere,' Jayme pointed out. 'And you can't go out to work, not with Leonie...' She had no need to go on.

Leonie was eight years old, and had been a difficult child almost from the day she was born. She was a sickly, clinging child who, when ill, wanted her mother, and when she was well, whether from fear of being ill again no one really knew, could not bear her mother out of her sight. Under protest, she was taken to school, only to be deeply distressed should anyone but her mother be at the school gates to meet her when school was over.

Michelle, Jayme's other sister, was two years older than Leonie, and was different again. She seldom had a day's illness and, being the studious one of the three, when Leonie had one of her 'weepy turns', she would stare at her solemnly from behind her glasses and then quietly get on with whatever project was current.

Since Audrey Warren could not see any employer putting up with her frequent absences when her youngest daughter went down with whatever was prevalent at the time, she had to rule out going out to work to earn money to keep them financially afloat for the next six years. In any case, since it was not possible to totally ignore Leonie's fears and phobias, any job she did find would have to be local and of such hours as to enable her to be at the school gates morning and afternoon.

With her going out to work out of the question, however, but since money had to be found from somewhere, Jayme's mother came up with the next best thing.

'Now I know why I always wanted a big, rambling house,' she told her sixteen-year-old daughter, adopting a cheerful note. 'We'll take in paying guests.'

'Paying guests!' Jayme exclaimed, not liking the idea of strangers treating her home as their home one little bit, but trying her hardest not to show it.

'I think it's a great idea!' Audrey went on enthusiastically, though not fooling Jayme for a moment with her false brightness. 'We've two spare bedrooms, and if I move Leonie's bed into our—m-my room,' she faltered briefly, before going on, 'which will please her, that will enable us to have three paying guests. We could,' she ended optimistically, 'finish up quite rich.'

It did not turn out that way. For one thing, Audrey Warren was a stickler for giving good value for money. For another, having a house to run and three growing daughters to clothe and feed simply ran away with the money. But they survived.

Jayme did leave school, though. Somehow, for she knew she had been her father's favourite, now he was no longer there, the heart went out of her for further study. She found herself a clerical job, but, at her mother's insistence, she enrolled at the local technical college to take a secretarial course two evenings each week. When she was not attending college Jayme helped her mother with housework, cooking, or, with three paying guests to be looked after, not to mention that Leonie was more often than not 'off colour', whatever chore had risen to the top of the work-pile.

Over the next few years Jayme exchanged her clerical job for a secretarial one. She was thus able, either directly or indirectly, to contribute more to the home. For as her earnings increased she began to contribute, indirectly, extra to the household by buying something from her pay cheque which she knew either Michelle or Leonie needed.

Leonie was twelve when, though still with a tendency to be a 'mother's girl', she suddenly ceased falling victim to every minor ailment that was doing the rounds.

It had been in February this year, when Leonie was fourteen, that she had started making noises about maybe wanting her own room. Jayme had exchanged glances with her mother—her baby sister was growing up a little!

Michelle had been sixteen in March, and was getting good reports from school and was earmarked as university potential. It was shortly after Michelle's birthday, though, that one of their paying guests had left.

Audrey Warren was cogitating whether she could afford to let Leonie have the vacated room or if she would have to ask her if she'd mind hanging on until next January, when she could begin to draw her late husband's pension, when the headmaster of the town's exclusive boys' boarding school rang. Apparently his Italian language master had had to return to Italy on family business. The business, it seemed, would take some time, and while the headmaster had been able to find someone to cover him for the one term he would be away, the new and temporary Italian teacher would prefer to live away from the school. He had heard that she took in paying guests and, since Audrey was so well recommended, could she help?

'Leonie,' Audrey Warren addressed her when she came off the phone, 'do you think you could bear to wait a little while for your own room?'

Leonie stared seriously at her mother, then smiled a sweet smile, a smile that perhaps too held a hint of relief. 'Oh, all right then,' she agreed, as if reluctant.

Jayme and her mother spent a good part of the Easter holiday in spring-cleaning the recently vacated guest-room. Then Tusco Bianco came to live with them—and life, for Jayme, was never the same after that.

From the beginning it was plain that their Italian guest had eyes for no one but her. Countless were the times when he would waylay her on some pretext or other. At first, however, Jayme tried to keep a level head on her shoulders. She was not unused to men giving her a second look, for, without conceit, she was aware that she had inherited her mother's good looks.

However, she had certain responsibilities, she would remind herself time and again as April gave way to May. By the time May had advanced nearer to June, though, she was, while endeavouring to keep her feet firmly planted on the ground, so far weakened by

Tusco's look of hurt whenever she refused to go out with him that she began to fail to see why she was being so rigid. It wasn't as though by going out with him she would be neglecting to do her share of the work in the home. She had been out on dates before, and had always fitted those outings in with helping her mother. Anyhow, hadn't her mother remarked on more than one occasion that she should have more interest in activities outside the home?

Not that Tusco Bianco could be called an interest outside the home, but when Jayme finished arguing in favour of accepting his next offer of a date she very soon realised that she was more than a little interested in him.

She had been kissed before Tusco had kissed her. But when he kissed her, Jayme faced the fact that she felt warmer towards him than she had towards any man up till now.

Their relationship progressed rapidly after that. After that first kiss Tusco seemed to be always around some corner in the house, waiting to take her in his arms.

Time began to go by too swiftly. For in no time there were less than two weeks to go before Tusco was due to return to Italy. Then, as Jayme decided that she loved him—although, despite his ardent behaviour towards her, he had not actually said he loved her—there was less than a week to go before he would say goodbye to them.

It was during that week that Tusco again managed to get her on her own, and, although he still did not declare his love, he told her he did not know how, when the time came for him to go, he would be able to leave her.

'Oh, Tusco!' she cried, and had just been about to go into his embrace when Michelle had come looking for her.

'Can you help me with my homework, Jayme?' she asked, wearing a worried look.

'Me, help you?' Jayme teased, and, sending a special smile to Tusco, she went with her sister, because it was seldom that Michelle asked for help from anyone.

Then it was Tusco's last evening in England. He was busy in his room packing while Jayme stood in the kitchen ironing the shirt he had put out for laundering that morning.

'I'll just take this up to Tusco,' she told her mother as she finished and put the ironing board away.

'I'll take it to him!' Leonie, in one of her helpful moods, piped up.

'Let Jayme take it, love,' Audrey Warren said calmly, raising her eyes from the hem she was sewing on a dress for Michelle, and sending a caring glance to her eldest daughter. 'I rather wanted you to make the batter for a Yorkshire pudding,' she told Leonie. 'You did it so well the last time.'

Jayme looked gratefully at her mother. They had already eaten their main meal, and she knew for a fact that there was no need for anyone to make a Yorkshire pudding, since they had been going to have roast lamb tomorrow, not beef.

She left the room with the shirt and a couple of handkerchiefs she had just ironed over her arm, aware that she had no secrets from her mother.

'I was beginning to despair that you would ever come to see me!' Tusco exclaimed as he answered her knock on his door.

'I've brought your laundry.'

'Come in—come in,' said Tusco, taking his laundry from her and setting it down, then taking hold of her arm he drew her into his room. 'We're friends enough for us not to be formal—one either side of the door—no?'

'Yes—er—I mean, no.' In fact Jayme was not quite sure what she meant, for Tusco was looking passionately at the curve of her mouth.

'How am I going to live without you?' he declared suddenly, and just as suddenly he pulled her into his arms.

Time had stood still a little for Jayme. Then, in between passionate kisses, Tusco, after an all-seeing look into her receptive sea-green eyes, was thrilling her by saying he could *not* live without her—and that she had to be his.

'You—want to—marry me?' she gulped out the question and was crushed to him in an embrace where, though she could not see his face, he confirmed that he wanted her to belong to him.

Passion soared between them, and Tusco begged her to wait for him, and told her his intention to labour all hours the sooner to enable him to send for her.

Then, as she looked at him with love in her eyes, he smiled, and had sidled her over to the bed. 'Let me have the one very special memory to keep me alive while I wait for you to come to me,' he pleaded.

'You—mean...?' Jayme swallowed

'If you love me...' he whispered.

'But...' she began hesitantly.

'Oh, my darling,' he cried, and Jayme was not so sure that there weren't tears in his eyes, 'can you let me return to Italy with our love unsealed?'

'But . . .' she said again as she tried to take a grip on a stray strand of sanity—that stray, faint something which said that this wasn't right.

'My darling, my darling,' Tusco cried brokenly, urgently, 'will you not prove your love for me? Will you not . . .' he went on to plead, but broke off as, just then, they both heard the sound of someone tapping at his bedroom door.

Hurriedly, and a degree guiltily, it had to be admitted, Jayme pulled out of his arms. Swiftly she went over to the door—but someone had started to turn the handle just as she got there.

'Oh!' exclaimed Leonie in slight surprise as she pushed the door inwards and saw her sister standing there, and not Tusco as she had expected. Then she went on cheerfully, 'I found this hanky on the stairs. Is it Tusco's?'

'Er—yes, it is,' Jayme answered, taking it from her and going to put it with the other clean laundry. 'It must have fallen off the top as I . . .'

'That's what I thought,' Leonie butted in brightly, and going over to Tusco, 'Do you want any help with your packing?' she offered willingly, and Jayme knew then what that faint 'something' had been earlier, which had said that it was not right that she give herself to Tusco.

It was a joy to her to know that Tusco wanted to marry her. But how could she prove her love to him in the way he asked with her mother so close by? How could she give herself in such a way when she had not one but two impressionable younger sisters in the house? Sisters who, it had to be said, despite their mother's lectures on always knocking on the guest-room doors and *waiting*, might well forget, and walk in without thinking.

Reminded of certain aspects of her responsibilities to her family, Jayme, shooing Leonie with her, left Tusco's room and went downstairs to wait for him to come to her when he would.

It was later that evening, when her mother tactfully went to bed, that Jayme and Tusco made their plans. At first, though, Tusco again grew passionate, and again begged her to 'prove her love'. But, having remembered her responsibilities to her family, Jayme told him how she felt.

'But your sisters are safely in bed!' he protested.

That wasn't quite the point. 'It's not unknown for Michelle to come down for a glass of milk if she fancies one,' Jayme told him, and followed that up by explaining that proof that she loved him must surely lie in the fact that she wanted to marry him.

From there they discussed plans to marry the following year. And, when Tusco finally departed the following day, Jayme could see that he looked as distraught at their parting as she felt.

There then followed a period of Jayme writing to him several times a week, and of watching for the postman for the letters which Tusco had said he would write. When not so much as a postcard came through the post from him in that first month, Jayme got seriously worried. Was he all right? Was he working so hard, the sooner for them to be together, that he had made himself ill? Or—as doubt crept in—had Tusco changed his mind about her?

Immediately she was ashamed of such thoughts. Oh, how could she think such a thing? Tusco loved her, he had said so over and over again that last night of his time in England, and she must never lose sight of that.

Perhaps he hadn't been able to find the work he wanted, and perhaps *he* was ashamed. Recalling how Tusco had told her that he wanted to give up teaching and, like one or two of his friends, turn to journalism, Jayme wondered if perhaps he was ashamed to write and tell her that he couldn't get any newspaper to take him on. Oh, it couldn't be that, could it?

Jayme decided that that could not be the answer as she also thought back to how he had declared that, in the event of not getting the work he wanted, he would take on any work he could, and work any hours he could, the sooner to see her again.

When two months went by since his return to Italy, though, Jayme felt she could bear the stress no longer. Though it was her mother who finally showed her what she must do. Audrey Warren had been fully acquainted with her daughter's plans, but when on Saturday Jayme came back from the postbox and it was clear from her expression that there was no communication from Italy that day either, her mother quickly found her two other daughters something to do elsewhere. Then she turned to the young woman who had been of value beyond price when her husband had been taken from her, and who had never failed her.

'Jayme,' she said, her manner, her tone, determined, 'if you haven't rung an airline within the next ten minutes to book a flight to Italy, then I shall do it for you.'

'You think I should go to see Tusco?'

'Yes,' her mother replied firmly. 'I do.'

'But I can't afford it!'

'Yes, we can!' her mother replied, and somehow they had.

Jayme recalled the fear she had nursed on that flight that she might discover that Tusco had been involved in a motor accident and could be in hospital. Or even . . .

Suddenly her thoughts were broken into as the engine of one of the many cars parked in the area near the lakeside where she was sitting sprang to life.

She glanced to where, some way up to her left, a car was reversing out. Her gaze was still on that spot when at once a lucky, and attractive, young woman straight away grabbed the parking spot.

Jayme observed that the car the woman was driving had a roof rack of the type used for toting sailboards around. She turned back to contemplate the lake. Clearly the woman had arrived at this prearranged time to pick up her man friend.

Nor, she further observed, did the man friend intend to keep her waiting for very long. For, if she wasn't mistaken, as she espied a distant sailboard making for the shore, it seemed that its occupant would end up close to where the woman was waiting.

Solemn-eyed, Jayme watched as the small figure on the sailboard grew larger. How she wished the man who was getting closer and closer was Tusco. But it wasn't Tusco; where *he* was, lord only——

Abruptly all thought left Jayme. For as man and sailboard came near to the rocky shallows, and as the man went to dismount, she saw, hardly daring to believe it, that—it *was* Tusco!

It was Tusco, her brain repeated. He hadn't had an accident, as she had sometimes imagined. He wasn't ill or in hospital. But, looking the very picture of health, he was here!

He was standing in the shallows, but had not seen her yet. Indeed, he was not even looking in her direction. He had a smile on his face, though, and, as relief and excitement at seeing him flooded her, Jayme half left her seat and opened her mouth to call his name.

She did not, however, call his name. For her relief and excitement were abruptly shattered. Incredulously, barely able to credit what her eyes were telling her, she saw Tusco leap eagerly from the rocks to the more even ground of the crazy-paving of the promenade, while at the same time the attractive woman who had just arrived swiftly left her car. In the next instant the two—regardless that he had just come out of the water—were tightly locked in a lovers' embrace.

Shock took a firm hold of Jayme as, still not believing what her eyes were telling her, she just stood and stared as the man she believed to be her fiancé continued to kiss the woman in his arms. Totally shattered, she watched as the two, oblivious to who was around, made a meal of each other. There could be little doubt that they were lovers.

The amorous pair were still oblivious to anyone who might be watching as Jayme went to step forward, maybe to confront him—she didn't know. But her pride suddenly took over.

She had no clear recollection of what happened after that, save for some vague notion of turning about and hurrying off in an opposite direction. It seemed paramount then that Tusco should never know she had flown from England in pursuit of him.

She crossed the road without knowing it. And, bent on hiding away, she hurried up an alleyway. Then, ignoring the fact that she found herself climbing a very steep and curving hill, she sped on. Tusco must not see her! He must not know that she had come here—that she had believed his lies when he had told her he loved her, and would until death. On and on she went, climbing up a steep and winding road.

Suddenly she was attacked by a stitch in her side, and, as exhaustion slowed her, she paused in her mad flight to realise that, instinctively, she had picked up her suitcase and had lugged it with her without even being aware of it. At any other time it would have been no wonder to her that, with the handicap of her suitcase—not to mention the steepness of the hill—she should feel exhausted. But she was not thinking about such things. All she was thinking of was that Tusco must not see her.

Suddenly she heard the full-throated roar of a car's engine, as the driver changed gear to tackle the steepness of the winding hill. But her thoughts were still intent on avoiding Tusco as in her panic she forgot entirely that traffic in Italy drove on the opposite side of the road from traffic in England. Automatically she flicked her glance to her right, then darted to cross the road.

The next thing she heard was the furious blast of someone thumping a car horn. Startled, she jerked her head to the left. Horrified, she made out the sleek black shape of a Ferrari. The driver did not stand a chance of missing her! Nor did he.

CHAPTER TWO

A CLOCK nearby chimed the quarter-hour. Jayme opened her sea-green eyes and found herself looking straight into the handsome and aristocratic face of a dark-eyed man who appeared to be stooping over her. He asked her something in rapid and urgent Italian, and she realised she liked the quality of his voice.

She closed her eyes again; she felt disorientated, yet strangely comfortable. The voice came again, more urgently this time, but she still had no clue to what he was saying—and she wanted to go to sleep.

Again the man with the handsome looks spoke urgently to her. Then a gentle hand came to cup the side of her face. Jayme turned her head into that hand; it was warm, and she felt reassured from his touch— secure somehow.

She breathed in deeply, for the moment content. *'Signorina!'* the voice insisted, and Jayme sighed. She wished he would go away. Though if he went away he would take that comforting hand with him.

Resignedly, she opened her eyes again. 'I can smell mint,' she told him, and thought his look of surprise must stem from the fact that he had not expected her to say anything of the sort.

'You're English!' he exclaimed. Then he smiled, a warm and pleasant smile, and Jayme was momentarily hypnotised by his perfect teeth.

Then suddenly she remembered that she knew another Italian male who had teeth that were nearly as perfect. 'I . . .' she started to say as she hurriedly tried to sit up.

She had moved too quickly, however, and everything began to swim crazily, and it took all the willpower she could find not to faint.

'Lie quietly for a while,' the Italian switched easily to English to instruct her, and, most peculiarly, all Jayme could think as he removed his hand from her face and pushed her gently back down again was that his pleasant voice had barely a trace of accent when he spoke her tongue.

'I don't speak Italian,' she heard her own voice volunteer the information apropos nothing. Then, as her eyes began to focus again, 'I feel all right,' she lied. But it seemed that he fully realised she was lying, for he smiled. 'What's wrong with me?' she asked him, though oddly she felt no panic.

'You tried to walk through my car' he replied, 'and came off second best.'

'The—Ferrari?'

'You remember?' he asked, and looked pleased.

By then, though, other memories, memories she did not want, were starting to intrude—were starting to bombard her. 'Where am I?' she asked him swiftly, and frowned, looking far from pleased.

'Since you appear to have no bones broken, I carried you in here out of the way of the traffic,' he explained, his eyes fixed firmly on her face and taking in her every changing expression.

'Er—thank you,' she murmured, and glanced around, to see that she appeared to be in some kind of park. She noticed her case nearby and everything came flooding back, including Tusco's recent treachery, and she started to get on her dignity. 'Thank you too for—for attending to me,' she went on jerkily as, this time taking it more slowly, she insisted on sitting up. 'I'm sorry if—er—if I've done any damage to your car,' she went on as she spotted her shoulder-bag and stretched out a hand for it. 'You've been m-more than k-kind.' She stood up—only to find that her legs did not seem ready yet to obey the messages she was sending to her brain. 'Oh!' she cried and, without having realised that the Italian had risen to his feet too—or that he was tall and that he towered over her—she suddenly collapsed up against him, with her face buried against his broad chest.

That was when she discovered that he was a man of action. For instead of putting her to lie down again, this time he picked her up in his arms as if she weighed nothing, although she was fairly tall too, and he strode with her from the park. She had some notion that they were again on the public highway—then the man, who seemed to have taken over, was halting where a long, black luxurious Ferrari was parked.

She was inside the car and the car was in motion before Jayme, willing herself to stay conscious, found sufficient strength to protest. 'Where are you taking me?' she asked.

'Not far, I promise you,' he replied soothingly. 'I've a villa I sometimes use near here. I should like a doctor to take a look at you.'

'But . . .' Jayme tried to argue. Then she discovered that she did not seem to be able to concentrate on any one thing for very long, and instead of going on to tell him, as she had intended, that she did not want to see a doctor, she found herself asking, 'Who are you?'

'My name is Nerone Mondadori di Vallanetto,' he replied formally, and turned to give her a reassuring look, then added, 'But you must call me Nerone.'

'Thank you,' she said a little vaguely. 'My name's Jayme Warren.'

'*Molto lieto*, Jayme,' he said lightly, and something inside Jayme smiled at his 'How do you do'.

'Fine,' she told him, then realised that they had reached his villa. She failed to comprehend very much at all after that, though, because her legs still seemed to belong to somebody else, and it was thanks to the Italian's superb physique that he had little trouble in extracting her from the car and carrying her inside.

'Rosa!' she heard him call, then she grew disorientated again.

She was only half aware of being carried to a sumptuously furnished bedroom. She surfaced a little, though, when a short and plump woman of mature years started to undress her and put her into bed.

'No!' she cried, but she had no idea of what she was protesting about.

'*Signore!*' she heard the woman call, then Nerone Mondadori was in the room too, and suddenly everything seemed all right again.

Without knowing it, Jayme caught hold of his hand. His grip tightened over hers and she felt that same sense of reassurance she had felt from the feel of his hand before. She was still holding on to his hand when she closed her eyes and went to sleep.

Her sleep was shortlived, however, for in next to no time, it seemed, there was another Italian male in the room. 'This is Dr Prandelli,' Nerone Mondadori introduced a fatherly-looking man. 'He will take good care of you,' he promised, and went from the room to send the short and plump woman in.

Dr Prandelli did not speak English as well as Nerone Mondadori did, but although his speech was very much slower, his questions were not difficult to follow.

He examined her for broken bones, cuts or abrasions. Then he shone a light in her eyes and asked her if she hurt anywhere. 'I feel fine,' she told him. And, at his old-fashioned look, 'Just—tired,' she admitted.

'Um-mmm,' murmured the doctor, which told Jayme precisely nothing. Then he was straightening up from the bed and telling her, 'There is no need for me to come and see you again, but,' he smiled a wicked smile. 'I will.'

His wicked smile, Jayme discerned, was harmless, so she smiled back at him. He had gone from the room, however, before her intelligence awakened. She should have told him not to bother to call again, she realised. She wouldn't be here for him to call to see again. Once she had got her head together, she would be leaving. Nerone Mondadori di Vallanetto had been very good to her as it was. She really just could not take advantage of his hospitality any longer.

She opened her mouth to tell him as much when, soon after Doctor Prandelli had gone, Nerone came to see her. At least, she opened her mouth to tell him her feelings and, most oddly, heard herself enquire, 'I heard you call "Rosa"—is Rosa your wife? I don't think I've met her yet.'

Belatedly she realised that maybe her question to this well-to-do Italian might seem impertinent, but he did not look in any way offended. He told her pleasantly, 'I'm not married, Jayme,' and, while part of her befuddled brain recognised that he seemed to be around thirty-five or six, and she realised that he would be something of a catch—should any female be up that early in the morning—his pleasant look became a grin as he told her, 'But you have met Rosa.

She's my housekeeper—the woman who helped you to bed.'

'Oh,' murmured Jayme, then remembered what she had meant to tell him. 'It was very good of—Rosa. Perhaps you would thank her for me. But I'll leave shortly. As soon as...' She broke off as his expression darkened.

'Leave!' he said toughly, and as if he thought she had just made a most outrageous suggestion. 'But I cannot allow you to leave!' he told her forcefully.

'Cannot, *signore*?' she queried, but the hands of tiredness had started to reach out for her again.

'What sort of a man do you think I am,' he demanded, 'that I should almost run you over and then, before you recover your full senses, should then proceed to allow you to leave my home?'

'But...' she tried to protest.

'Enough!' Nerone cut her off, and there was something in his voice with which Jayme saw there was no arguing. She tried just the same, weak though her effort was.

'It's not right,' she told him, but her voice was drowsy, and not at all as assertive as she had meant it to be.

The next thing she knew was that she was again waking from sleep and that Nerone Mondadori was no longer in her room. Someone was in her room, though. That someone was his housekeeper, Rosa, and she was bending over the suitcase which Jayme recognised as her own, and *unpacking it*!

'Excuse me!' Jayme made her presence known, and was ready to tell Rosa not to unpack any more because she would have to pack all the housekeeper had unpacked in a very little while. But she did not get the chance to try to get across any of what she wanted to say, because the woman had turned at the sound of her voice and, with a smile in her direction, went quickly out of the room.

She was soon back, however, and Jayme swiftly realised, as Nerone entered the room with her, that Rosa had gone to tell him that she was awake.

'You have more colour in your pale cheeks,' he observed as she struggled to a sitting position.

'Rosa is unpacking my things,' Jayme responded.

'You wished to do it yourself?' he queried, seeming slightly puzzled. 'But you are not well...'

'It's not that I mind her doing it,' Jayme corrected him. 'Well, I do—that is...' she broke off, 'I'm confused,' she told him frustratedly.

'Which is why you will stay in my home until you're feeling better,' he told her, and came and sat on the side of the bed. He succeeded in confusing her even more when she saw his eyes rest on the bareness of her shoulder where the strap of her nightdress had slipped down.

'But I should be in a hotel,' Jayme struggled out of her confusion to tell him. 'I can't just offload myself on to you and...'

'What a proud young woman you are!' Nerone teased her suddenly, and wrought more havoc in her when he stretched out long, sensitive fingers to her naked shoulder. Abruptly she pulled back, then felt ridiculous when, his intention all at once plain, all that Nerone did was to pull the bed sheet up over her uncovered shoulder as though it was of some concern to him that she did not catch a chill on top of everything else.

'You don't understand...' she tried.

'I understand perfectly that you want to make me feel more guilty than I already do,' he cut her off.

Startled, Jayme stared at him. 'You feel guilty?' she questioned. 'But I didn't give you any chance of missing me when I walked in front of you the way I did!'

'It was fortunate that because of the winding road I was not driving at all fast,' he replied, halted, then said, 'But I thought no one ever remembered the events immediately prior to an accident?'

How she wished that were true. What a gullible, idiotic fool she had been over Tusco! Whatever had made her think that the love she and Tusco had was different, and that his failure to write meant there must be something wrong—other than the obvious?

'What is it?' Nerone's voice, sharp and enquiring, brought Jayme swiftly back to the present, to realise that her face must be very expressive. 'What thoughts make you look so sad?' he demanded to know.

'Nothing—none,' she told him, knowing that wild horses would not drag from her the information that she had that day discovered herself jilted.

'You have a headache?' he persisted. 'Dr Prandelli said you might suffer with a bad head before nightfall.'

'I'm fine, honestly. Not a headache in sight,' Jayme assured him, then found that Nerone Mondadori was like a terrier with a bone when he suspected something was amiss.

'If you're worried about your hotel,' he hit upon another reason for her look of pensiveness, 'then nothing will be more simple than for me to telephone and cancel your reservation.'

'I'm not booked in anywhere,' Jayme told him unthinkingly.

'You were leaving Torbole?' he enquired, but her thoughts were floating elsewhere.

'I only arrived this morning,' she replied woodenly, again without thinking. She should never have come, she realised that now.

By sheer force of his will her eyes seemed to be drawn back to Nerone, and she saw that he was giving her very close scrutiny. She rather suspected then, as his eyes scanned her wan features, that, still terrier-like, he was about to demand just what she was doing in Torbole, with a suitcase, but with no hotel booking made. Her chin jutted a tiny fraction as she willed herself away from the lethargy she was feeling, and silently sought for some polite way of telling him to mind his own business.

She discovered, though, that her efforts in that department would not be necessary, because suddenly Nerone was getting up from the bed, saying gently, 'You're still in shock, little one, I think,' and, while every scrap of aggressive feeling drained from her at his gentle tone, 'Allow Rosa to help you to bathe and return to bed,' he went on quietly. 'Then I suggest an early supper and a couple of the tablets the doctor left with me. We will talk in the morning,' he finished calmly.

Jayme was not so sure that there was anything for them to talk about in the morning. But when Nerone had left her, it somehow seemed easier just then to go along with the first part of his suggestion. Somehow it seemed less of an effort to let someone else take charge.

She was glad to find, though, that the strength had returned to her limbs when, with Rosa in attendance, she went and had a bath. Maybe I am in shock, she mused as she returned to her bed and ate the light supper which Rosa had prepared, then dutifully swallowed two tablets.

She had received not one shock but two that day, she reflected as she lay down and pulled the light bed-covers up around her. After waiting anxiously all this time for news of Tusco, it had been a mind-stunning blow to witness with her own eyes the fickleness of the love he said he felt for her. Jayme tucked the pillow more comfortably into her neck. The other shock she had received, of course, had been to turn at the blast of a car horn and see the black roaring monster of Nerone's Ferrari leaping to gobble her up.

How he had managed to halt his car before it had flattened her, she had no idea. Proof, though, that he must have literally stood on his brakes lay in the fact that although he had been unable to prevent his car from knocking her down, she had no crushed or broken bones to show for the collision. It had been good of him to... Her thoughts grew woolly as she forgot what she had been thinking about. Another minute passed, then she went to sleep.

Jayme stirred in her sleep as daylight filtered through the night sky on Wednesday morning. Immediately, as twinges of pain attacked, she knew she had been in a motor accident. She went to sit up, but, having moved too quickly, she was swiftly made to realise that she wasn't rushing anywhere that day. Gingerly she propelled her stiffened body in the direction she wanted it to go. Having made it to a sitting position, however, she decided that she felt better lying down.

The next time she awoke it was to hear the sound of someone tapping on her bedroom door. 'Come in,' she called, but did not make the mistake this time of hurrying to sit up.

'*Buon giorno,*' Rosa greeted her cheerfully, having been about to 'come in' anyway, Jayme guessed, since the housekeeper's English was about as brilliant as her Italian.

There followed a whole stream of incomprehensible Italian from the plump little lady, which, as Jayme struggled to a sitting position, she suspected meant that Rosa was asking her how she was that morning. *'Molto, molto bettero,'* she made up her Italian as she went along, realising that she had just murdered that beautiful language when Rosa stared uncomprehendingly at her.

At that point, however, Nerone Mondadori came through the open bedroom door. 'So you're feeling much, much better this morning?' he queried, quickly translating what Jayme had been trying to convey to his housekeeper, who, smiling, placed the cup of tea from the tray she carried on the bedside table, and went away.

'Yes,' Jayme answered Nerone. Observing the way his glance took in every detail of her from her sleep-tousled blonde hair to her arms holding down the bedcovers, she saw he was giving her his undivided attention. 'I slept like a top,' she informed him. She saw, strangely, with more interest than she would have expected, the way the corners of his mouth twitched, and realised that he was so amply at home with her language that he had no need to ask what 'like a top' meant. 'I'll get up presently,' she told him, having firmly decided that she wasn't a bit interested in whether his grin looked imminent or not.

Abruptly, though, his tone changed, and there was not so much as a trace of a grin about him as he rapped, *'That* is not possible!'

'What?' she queried, in some astonishment, having announced that she would leave her bed, and not ready to have him or anyone else set about changing her

decisions for her. She realised then that, even if her
body was starting to feel the after-effects of yesterday,
her head had cleared to make her once more the sort
of person who was more normally in charge of herself.

'Forgive me,' Nerone apologised, and with such
charm that her ruffled feathers were immediately
smoothed. 'But from the bruising that is starting to
show on you, I feel that you cannot be so *"molto,
molto bettero"* as you would have Rosa believe.' His
grin did come out then, and as her heart hurriedly
doubled a beat—which Jayme put down to being all
part and parcel of her body choosing today to put in
a protest about yesterday's accident—Nerone went on,
'The good doctor expressly told me that you should
spend today resting in your bed.'

'He did?' she exclaimed, startled, though her
thoughts were more on the fact that it seemed unthinkable to her that she should trespass on this man's
hospitality any more than she had done already.

Solemnly, Nerone nodded. 'It is either here or a
hospital bed, I fear,' he told her.

'Hospital!' Jayme exclaimed, her eyes growing
wide. 'But I feel all right this morning,' she said with
more fervour than accuracy, and in so doing, she made
an abstracted movement which jarred her body. Too
late to control it, she winced.

'Are you sure about that?' Nerone, who, she was
fast realising, never missed a thing, enquired.

'I don't want to be a nuisance,' she mumbled.

'The only nuisance you will be will be to my conscience if you will not allow me to do all in my power
to make you well again,' he replied gallantly.

Jayme looked at him and noticed that his hair was
several shades lighter in colour than the night-black
shade of most of the Italians she had come across.

She then realised that she was staring at him, and quickly switched her gaze, then brought her concentration back to the subject under discussion. 'It won't make any difference to your conscience if I repeat that I in no way hold you responsible for my accident yesterday?'

'None,' he answered and, the matter settled as far as he was concerned, he told her, 'Drink your tea, then Rosa will be here to help you.'

Jayme was glad of Rosa's assistance when later, her arms and body showing most definite signs of bruising, she had a hot bath. She returned to her bed and Rosa went and opened the french doors in her room to let the sunlight stream in.

Thereafter the morning seemed a busy time of eating breakfast and of sleeping, of waking to find Nerone in her room with all the latest English magazines, and of feeling that she was being very much spoiled.

Doctor Prandelli called to see her around noon. He took her bruises in his stride and pronounced that she would be feeling more herself tomorrow. Once his examination was over and Rosa left the room the doctor looked ready to dispose himself for a good long chat. But he had no sooner settled himself in a bedside chair than Nerone had come and seemed to want a private word with him.

Lunch consisted of a delicious soup followed by steak and salad, then chocolate pudding. By that time Jayme's strength was rapidly returning, so that she started to feel a fraud. '*Molto grazie*, Rosa,' she thanked the housekeeper, and wished she knew the Italian for 'simply delicious.'

She was wide awake when later that afternoon Nerone came to pay her a visit. 'How are you?' he asked formally.

'I'm getting better by the minute and feeling a fraud to be waited on,' Jayme replied as she cricked her neck to look up at his lofty height. She wished he would sit down.

It was almost as if he read her mind, for the next moment he was hooking the cream and gold brocade bedroom chair nearer the bed. Before he sat down, though, he brought from behind his back a small plate of delicious-looking grapes. 'I have it on good authority,' he told her solemnly, 'that one never goes visiting the indisposed in your country without grapes.'

Taken very much aback, Jayme stared at him for several moments. Then, as she espied that there was very much of a twinkle in the dark velvety solemnity of her host's eyes, humour bubbled to the surface, and, for the first time in an age, she burst out laughing.

She thought afterwards that perhaps Nerone must have been fed up with her unsmiling countenance. In any event, he seemed arrested by the musical sound of her light and spontaneous laughter.

'Molto grazie,' she told him as she sobered and he sat down. Then, 'Did your very good authority also tell you that it is customary in my country for the bearer of the grapes to sit and eat them during the visit?'

'I confess, my education is incomplete,' he replied, eyeing her pleasantly.

'Did you grow them yourself?' asked Jayme, as the thought struck her. 'The grapes, I mean,' she added, realising, without consciously ever having thought about it, that the car he drove, this sumptuous villa and everything else about him decreed that he must be a man of some wealth. 'Do you have a vineyard?' she enquired.

As if charmed by her innocent, eager questions, Nerone smiled. 'I'm afraid not,' he told her. 'I make my living in industry in Turin. I've some factories there,' he explained, as if having 'some factories' was an everyday sort of thing. 'There are vineyards near here in Trentino,' he went on to assist her education, 'but I fear that the wine grapes are not the same as these.'

For the next ten minutes of Nerone's visit they conversed pleasantly on inconsequential matters, until suddenly something struck Jayme and she changed the subject to question, 'If your living—your business is in Turin, then...' She broke off and had a vague memory of his telling her that he 'sometimes used' this villa. 'Are you on holiday?' she asked him urgently.

'Even industrialists rest sometimes,' he responded.

'Oh,' Jayme wailed, 'I'm spoiling it for you!'

'Spoiling...what is this?' asked Nerone, clearly having no idea what she was getting at.

'I'm spoiling your holiday!' she enlightened him. 'Oh, I'm so sorry,' she apologised, knowing that one did not get to be wealthy without working very hard for it.

'Do not apologise,' Nerone commanded her sternly. 'It is I who should apologise to you for spoiling *your* holiday.'

It was a moment, Jayme knew, when she could have told him that she was not in Italy on holiday. But even though some sixth sense was telling her that there was a subtle degree of probing in Nerone's last sentence she could not tell him the true reason for her being in Italy. She had pushed Tusco and the insincerity of his love to the back of her mind. She was still most firmly of the view that no one was going to know anything about it.

'What do you normally do on holiday?' she asked Nerone instead.

For long seconds he did not answer, but stared at her as though trying to glean what went on in her head. Then casually he shrugged, 'Whatever happens to appeal at the time,' he replied. 'A little sailing, perhaps, some...'

'Have you done any sailing this holiday?' she interrupted him to question.

'This holiday I was foolish enough to bring some work with me. So far,' he said with likeable self-mockery, 'all I've seen is the inside of my study.'

'You must rest sometimes,' Jayme told him sternly, and felt her heart flutter absurdly when, as though her manner, her words, had amused him, this time he laughed. She realised that she liked the sound.

He was soon over his amusement, however, though his voice remained relaxed and easy. 'Do you have an occupation, Jayme?' he wanted to know.

'Lord, yes,' she replied, and started to feel more relaxed herself now that she could see he had little or no interest in her reasons for being in Italy. 'I've worked since I was sixteen,' she felt relaxed enough to tell him.

'You finished your formal education early,' he murmured.

His remark had been a passing comment only, Jayme thought, and required no reply. Which made it a mystery to her why she should suddenly find herself telling him. 'My father died, and my mother had enough worry about in keeping the home going and in feeding and clothing my two younger sisters without having the added burden of me going on to full-time further education. But in any case, I wanted to leave school.'

She was aware of Nerone's look quiet upon her. But she was ready to defend her father up to the hilt when the aristocratic-looking Italian questioned, 'Your father died leaving you unprovided for?'

'We were provided for!' she replied instantly, sharply. 'It was just that, because he hadn't expected to die so young, there was a time lapse on his pension payable to his widow. It becomes payable next January,' she told him stonily.

'Put your loyal hackles down, little one,' Nerone instructed her calmly. 'I'm on your side.'

Jayme gave him a slightly ashamed look at her outburst. Then, probably because Nerone had been so kind to her, she found herself telling him more than she meant to as she excused, 'My father was a wonderful man, and we all loved him very much. Especially my mother, of course,' she added, thinking back to the devotion she remembered her parents had shared.

'Did your mother too find herself an occupation after your father's death?' Nerone questioned quietly. 'Or did she perhaps already have a career?'

This time Jayme did not see any hint of blame to her father in his remark, and she relaxed again to answer, 'My mother felt her career was in the home, and felt quite fulfilled and not at all downtrodden at being—as my father put it—in the top ranks of diplomacy and management on the home front.'

'Your home must have been a happy one,' Nerone observed.

'It was,' Jayme agreed, and after pausing for a moment she realised that he was waiting politely for her to answer his question of whether her mother had found herself an occupation outside the home when her husband had died. 'My mother and I discussed her going out to work,' she went on, certain that she was receiving encouraging vibes from him and, for no reason at all, feeling, strangely, that she could confide in him. 'But my youngest sister, Leonie, was at that time a nervous, timid child, and needed the security of knowing that her mother was at home and would be at her school to meet her when she had finished her classes for the day. So we realised that it was impossible for my mother to go out to work.'

'But at sixteen you could not possibly earn sufficient to support your family!' Nerone exclaimed, and Jayme laughed lightly.

'Of course I couldn't,' she had to agree. 'Which was why my mother decided that we must take in paying guests.'

'I've a feeling,' Nerone remarked after some moments, 'that your mother was not so happy with what she had decided she must do.'

Jayme smiled at him for his insight. 'She wasn't,' she confirmed. 'But we have a big rambling house, which she loves and didn't want to leave; to take in boarders to keep us afloat until my father's pension became payable was a sacrifice she decided she must make.'

'The same way you sacrificed your full-time education,' Nerone inserted.

'Oh, tosh!' Jayme scorned, then swiftly. 'I'm sorry, Nerone, that wasn't very polite, was it?' she apologised, and thought what a nice person he was when he smiled the most charming smile at her. 'I didn't finish with school completely,' she found herself telling him. 'I attended a secretarial course two evenings a week.'

'So,' he documented, 'you left school, and started work. You learned to be a secretary two evenings a week, and on the other evenings you came home to help your mother with the extra work brought on by the intruders into your home.'

'I never said that!' Jayme exclaimed.

'You didn't have to,' he replied. 'I cannot picture you returning to your home and sitting down to take your ease while your mother worked on,' said this man who, an astonished Jayme realised, had greater powers of perception than anyone she had ever met. Until yesterday, she had been unknown to him, and yet now... Her thoughts broke off as Nerone continued, 'Would you deny your ability to cook and housekeep—when it must be you who takes over when your mother perhaps is occasionally feeling unwell, or has need to escort one of your sisters to a function outside the home?'

'Do you ever get it wrong?' Jayme queried, slightly awestruck.

'Seldom,' grinned Nerone, then, getting up from his chair, he selected a grape from the rinsed bunch he had given her and, looking down into her beautiful but still pale face told her, 'I think you should try to sleep for a little while.' And with a long, easy stride, he went quietly from her room.

Jayme did not go to sleep when he had gone. Nerone Mondadori di Vallanetto had given her far too much to think about. It was no wonder to her that he was the man at the head of 'some factories'; he was 'that sort of a man'. She realised, though, that she quite liked him, but she could in no way comprehend how he had been able to get so much out of her. Normally, she was most private about her family. Normally, however, she mused, she didn't go charging about crashing into Ferraris!

She forgot Nerone for a moment as the memory of that accident brought back memories of just why she had been charging about. She had been haring up that winding hill as if by doing so she would get away from the scene she had witnessed of Tusco with his new love down by the lake.

Now that she knew what she knew, Jayme was amazed at her own credulity. The writing had already been on the wall in the shape of Tusco not answering one of her letters. But she had been so blinded by all his protestations of love that she hadn't been able to see that his proposal had never been serious. With hindsight—knowing what she now did—only then did she see what a fool she had been.

Jayme dwelt for some time on her stupid gullibility. It was too late now, of course, to play back how Tusco had come to tell her of his love and how he had come to ask her to marry him. Too late now to realise what should have been plain then but hadn't—that all he had been interested in had been in trying to get her into bed!

It was useless to blame her lack of experience with the male sex on her failure to see what had been at the back of his 'marriage' proposal. Green—good grief, grass wasn't greener!

To face up to the fact that she had been an idiot to believe in Tusco the way she had was painful. To accept that she had been an even bigger fool to come to Italy looking for him was unpleasant. But, in coming to terms with Tusco Bianco's treachery, Jayme, deciding that he most plainly was not worth another thought, was bombarded by disquiet on another issue. An issue that had not been far from her mind all day—she should have rung home by now. Her worried mother would be waiting with growing agitation to hear from her.

Jayme fretted about what she should do for the best over the next couple of hours. Bobbing about in her head at the same time, too, was her own worry of somehow making it to the airport in Verona, and of getting back to England with all speed. Though, with her body sending spiteful spears of pain each time she moved, she shuddered at the thought of dressing and lugging her suitcase around.

Which meant, she saw, that she might need another day or so before she felt up to making that flight home. So what was she going to do about letting her mother know how things were at the 'Italian end'? And what, for goodness' sake, was she going to tell her about Tusco without making her more anxious than she was now?

When Rosa brought her dinner to her, Jayme had anguished for so long about her mother waiting uneasily, and with ears pitched, for the phone to ring, that she had no appetite for food.

'*Grazie*, Rosa,' she told her, as Rosa went to close the french doors. Then, because the housekeeper had gone to the trouble of cooking the meal, Jayme did her best to eat some of it. But it was no good, her appetite had gone completely, and when Rosa returned for her tray some while later, most of her dinner was untouched.

A fact which she was soon to learn had been reported to Rosa's master—and quickly too. For within minutes he had come striding into the bedroom. He was tall, authoritative and tough, as he looked keenly down at her sitting stiffly in bed.

'The look of fatigue about you has increased, not decreased as I hoped when I left you,' he observed, and demanded, 'What troubles you, Jayme?'

'Nothing,' she replied quickly. She had not been aware that she had been looking fatigued, though she was not surprised that she should seem so now—she felt quite frayed from worrying what to do for the best.

'You are in pain?' Nerone pressed.

'No,' she told him.

'Don't lie!' he clipped, and she saw stark aggression in him for the first time. Most plainly he was someone who, like her, didn't care for lies either.

'Very well then,' she snapped. 'I hurt—a little.'

'I'll get a doctor.' Having made up his mind on the instant, he was striding towards the door before, suddenly feeling exasperated by him, Jayme broke into hurried speech.

'I don't want a doctor!' she stated, her voice starting to rise in her urgency to stop him. 'I want to phone my mother!' she cried, her mind more on his high-handed manner than on what she was saying.

Abruptly Nerone halted. Then, as he turned, Jayme saw all sign of aggression leave him. In the next moment he had come back to stand by the bed and had lifted her right hand from the coverlet, keeping a hold of it in that way she found most comforting. 'Forgive me, Jayme,' he said gently. 'I should have thought of that myself.' Then, as if cursing his lack of consideration to her—when to her mind he had been the most considerate of hosts—he instructed, 'Wait but a moment more,' and returned her hand to the coverlet. 'I will bring a telephone to you.'

With that, and all before she could tell him that she wasn't after all so very sure about putting that call through to her mother, he had gone from her sight. Though, when in next to no time he had returned and was plugging in the phone near to the bedhead, Jayme realised that her conscience was going to bother her until she had put through her promised call to her parent.

'Here you are,' he murmured as with everything set for her to make her call he handed her the receiver. 'The telephone code to England is known to me. Give me your area code and number, and I'll dial it for you,' he offered, as if aware of the way her body creaked with every movement. Jayme told him the digits he needed, and watched as, leaving off the first 'O', he dialed her home number.

Nerone stepped away from the bed when his task was completed, but even though he went towards the door she was aware that he paused before leaving in case she required his assistance further, should there be anything at all wrong with the connection.

Then the fact that Nerone was there went from her mind as she heard the ringing tone, and realised she should be concentrating all her efforts on what she could possibly tell her mother that would make her less anxious about her than she was already. Then she heard her lovely parent's voice, and for a while she kept her mind solely on freeing her from any more stress.

'Hello, Mum,' she said brightly.

'Jayme!' Audrey Warren's already relieved tones came down the wire. 'Oh, love, I've been so worried about you! Are you all right?'

'I'm fine,' Jayme told her cheerfully, knowing that when she saw her would be time enough to tell her about her brush with Nerone's car.

'And Tusco?' her mother enquired. 'Was he ill, as you thought?'

Jayme remembered how much 'in fine fettle' Tusco had been the last time she had seen him. 'He's fine too,' she answered, and, in an attempt to avert more questions about her ex—and never was—fiancé, she asked, 'Are Michelle and Leonie all right?'

'Of course they are,' her mother assured her. 'But I'm more interested in you just now. Did Tusco say why he hadn't answered any of your letters?'

'He'd changed his address a couple of times,' Jayme replied, knowing that if she didn't want to cause her mother worse ferment she'd be better keeping quiet until she got home about the disillusionment that had awaited her in Italy. 'We met up in a place called Torbole,' she said brightly, and, finding that cheerful note again. 'Tusco's looking fit and happy, and...'

'Well, of course he's happy, dear,' her mother cut in. 'He's got you as his future bride—what more could a man wish for?' she said proudly, and went on to state, from her heart, 'You know, darling, don't you, that although we'll miss you dreadfully, you don't have to wait for my financial affairs to pick up if you want to advance your wedding date?'

'Oh, Mum!' Jayme cried, and had to fight really hard to keep up the pretence of there not being a cloud on her horizon. 'Actually, though, Tusco and I still don't plan to marry before next year...' She broke off as something remarkably like an explosion of extreme annoyance hit her ears. The sound was close by, and did not come from down the telephone. Swiftly Jayme realised that the sound had come from

Nerone, and belatedly she realised that, since she was prattling on on a very long-distance call on his phone, perhaps he had every right to be annoyed. 'I'll have to go,' she told her mother.

'All right, dear,' her parent replied. 'I feel better now that you've been in touch.'

Jayme was still saying her goodbyes as she returned the phone to its rest. Then, ready with her apologies but ready to also state that she would of course pay for the call, she looked up and over to where Nerone was standing.

She had, since she had been in Italy, been the receiver of one or two shocks. But, as her gaze rested on the tall, aristocratic Italian, Jayme had yet another shock. For all sign of the pleasant man she thought she was getting to know had gone.

'I'm...' she opened her mouth to begin her apology anyway, when Nerone Mondadori's look of furious outrage stopped her.

She then discovered that, as well as seeing nothing whatsoever wrong in listening to her conversation with someone else, this enraged-looking man did not hesitate to refer to it. But she was left absolutely flabbergasted when, nothing whatsoever inhibiting about his command of her language, he thundered furiously, 'Who in hell's name, *signorina*, is Tusco?'

CHAPTER THREE

BLANKLY, Jayme stared into the fierce glare of Nerone's eyes. Even without the fact that she was suddenly *'signorina'* and no longer the more friendly 'Jayme', she didn't need two looks at his incensed stance to know that something she'd done had infuriated him.

'I d-don't understand,' she stammered, doing her best not to be intimidated by the whole threatening look of him.

'You have a man friend here in Italy—in Torbole?' Nerone rapped for an answer.

'Well—sort of,' Jayme tried to answer honestly, not certain in the circumstances of Tusco's duplicity whether she wanted to claim him as a friend or not.

'He's your *lover*?' her host roared, and took an enraged step nearer the bed.

'No!' she denied sharply, most pleased that the vehemence of her reply halted Nerone just as it seemed he would come yet closer to her bed—he looked dangerous enough the four yards or so he was away, without coming any closer. 'Tusco and I knew each other in England. He lodged with us for a short while,' she began to explain quickly—only to be interrupted, her explanations not quick enough for Nerone Mondadori, apparently.

'You deliberately avoided answering my supposition that you were here on holiday,' he tossed at her angrily. 'No wonder you had no hotel accommodation booked—you followed this—man,' he spat the word, 'to Torbole intending to live with him. You . . .'

He seemed unstoppable in his rage, but Jayme was growing enraged too. *'I did not!'* she yelled, forcing her way in as she lost her temper in a way in which she had never done in her whole life. 'Before Tusco Bianco left England, he asked me to marry him,' she stormed on, her eyes flashing out her fury as she ignored the way Nerone's hands clenched at his sides. 'When . . .'

'This man asked you to marry him?' Nerone sliced in before she could get much further. 'You agreed to marry him?'

'It's why I wrote to him after he left England!' she slammed back, and charged on, 'When, in two months, not one of my letters was answered, I was naïve enough to think that it couldn't be because he hadn't meant his marriage proposal, but might be that he was overworking on account of his vow to labour night and day so that we could marry next year.'

'You're saying that he did not mean his marriage proposal?' Nerone barked toughly, and Jayme guessed from his grim expression that he was not enthralled with her blackening the character of one of his countrymen.

'That's what I'm saying,' she replied coldly.

'Why, then, did he ask you to marry him?' Nerone pressed.

'The answer to that has become obvious since I've been here,' Jayme retorted.

'Make it obvious to me,' he demanded, although Jayme could see no reason why she should.

When he continued to stare silently and icily at her, however, she found that his very silence was pushing her into making some reply. 'You're a man of the

world, *signore*,' she snapped bluntly, and a trace in-
solently, she had to own. 'Do I have to spell it out
for you?'

Oh, my hat! she thought a second later as she saw
the ice in his eyes go arctic, and a second after that
discovered that he was a man who clearly knew how
to hurt. 'You're saying that the only way he could get
you into bed was to propose marriage to you?' he
demanded.

'That's about it!' she confirmed coldly, and saw
the look in his eyes change instantly from being arctic
to a blazing inferno.

'So the two of you *are* lovers?' he snarled.

'No, we are *not*!' Jayme denied hotly, 'nor ever have
been, in the way *you* mean,' she stormed, and was so
angry she found herself blazing on. 'He wanted me
to prove my love "that way", but I couldn't, not with
my mother and my two innocent sisters in the house!'
Heavens, she fumed, how in the world had they ever
got on to this subject?

But the subject, she discovered, was not finished
yet, for she was fast finding that Nerone Mondadori
was not above asking anything he wanted to know—
no matter how personal!

'You've had other lovers, however?' he demanded.

And even as Jayme was thinking he could go to hell
before she'd answer, she heard herself flaring, 'When
would I get the chance?' Furious with him, furious
with herself, she looked away from him.

Nerone's voice was quieter, and a shade less tough,
as he enquired, 'Is this the first time you've been away
from your home?' It seemed he was ready to believe
her assertion that she couldn't give herself to any man
in her home.

'I'm still a virgin, if that's what you're asking,' she told him bluntly, wishing he would go away and leave her in peace.

'You love this man Bianco?' he rapped.

'There seems little point in my doing that,' she replied tartly.

'I agree,' he said icily. 'Yet you've just told your mother that you plan to marry him next year.'

'I couldn't tell her any of the awful things that have happened to me since I last saw her on Monday!' Jayme erupted. 'She's been worried enough about me since then without giving her more to worry about by telling her that my one and only sight of Tusco was down at the lakeside yesterday, when he was oblivious to anyone but the responding woman in his arms.'

'He didn't see you?'

'As far as he knows, I'm still in England,' she replied. 'I took off up the hill as soon as I'd taken in that "absence didn't make the heart grow fonder"— then I met you and your Ferrari.'

She came to a hostile end, and glared at him. Hostilely he glared back. Then, as if her last remark had reminded him that he and his car were all part of the trauma she had been through, and the cause of the external bruises she wore, he clamped his lips firmly together on any more acid he might have found, and told her in taut tones, 'I'll wish you *buona notte, signorina.*' With that he inclined his aristocratic head in her direction and strode swiftly from her room.

Jayme was still sitting, stunned, when a short while later Rosa, obviously on her master's instructions, came in with a warm bedtime drink.

'*Grazie*, Rosa,' said Jayme as the two exchanged goodnights, but Nerone's action in seeing to it that she had a milky drink to sustain her through the dark hours only succeeded in confusing her further.

'Complicated' did not begin to describe the man he was turning out to be, she mused tiredly. How anyone could change so instantly from being friendly and kind to the hostile monster Nerone had shown himself to be was beyond her. Perhaps it was all part and parcel of the Italian temperament, she cogitated, although, in all the three months Tusco had lived with them, she had never seen his rage ignite so spontaneously.

Not that she had ever seen Tusco in a rage, she reflected, then forgot Tusco for a while as she wondered what on earth her furious row with Nerone had been all about anyhow.

Realising that she felt quite exhausted, Jayme gingerly lay down in her bed, and, very much aware of her aches and pains, realised too that one needed to be fully fit to square up to her host.

Not that she had backed away, though. Certainly she had never known that there was so much temper in her. Yet still the question persisted—what had that dreadful row been all about? And how, when she had been positive that wild horses wouldn't get her to admit that the man she had come to Italy to see no longer wanted to marry her, had it come about that she had told Nerone almost everything there was to tell him! True, she had lost control of her temper at the time.

Jayme slept badly that night, for, apart from the fact that she was being stabbed by darts of pain each time she moved her limbs or her body more than a fraction, the unanswered question in her brain returned again and again to torment her.

By dawn, however, she had reached a couple of conclusions. One was that she must have made Nerone angry when he had realised from her end of the telephone conversation that she knew someone else in the area quite well, and yet had parked herself on him after the accident. Even when she recalled how it had seemed important to him that she should stay in his home to recover, it seemed the only conclusion which would fit.

Which brought her to her other conclusion. She was leaving. Spiteful darts of pain or no spiteful darts of pain, if she had to crawl out of there on her hands and knees, she would.

As it happened, though, her progress when she left her bed to go and take a bath was not as bad as that. She was quite able to walk upright. Although, with no one watching, she had to decide that there was no point in rushing. Slowly she made it to the bathroom, where she stripped off and viewed her bruised Technicolor body in the mirror with some disbelief. How on earth, without breaking something, had she amassed all that bruising?

Her progress seemed easier after a hot bath, but she still wasn't breaking any speed records when she returned to the bedroom and sorted through the wardrobe for something to wear.

She opted for white cotton trousers and a navy and white striped cotton top. The cotton top had long sleeves which nicely covered a large bruise on her right forearm.

Amazed that she should feel so exhausted when all she had done was to get herself bathed and dressed, Jayme decided she would pack her things later. First she had better check her financial position.

Taking her shoulder-bag, she went to the cream and gold bedroom chair and sat down. She checked through her money and calculated that she had enough funds to cause her no problems. All she needed was enough for a taxi ride to Verona airport, and once there she could start putting this whole dreadful episode behi...

Her thoughts ended in mid-air. Since she had her return to England in her mind, it was automatic that, having checked her finances, she should then assure herself that she had her passport ready. The problem was—she could not see it!

With more haste than thought for her still delicate body, Jayme emptied the contents of her bag out on to the bed. Her passport was not there! Systematically she put everything back in her bag piece by piece. It still wasn't there!

Next she tried to remember when she had last seen it. It was at Verona airport on Monday, she realised, and she could not remember having seen it since then.

She was just wondering what on earth she was to do now when, after tapping lightly on her door, Rosa came in with a cup of tea for her. *'Buon giorno, signorina,'* the housekeeper greeted her smilingly.

Jayme thanked her for the tea, and managed to return the smile, then tried out some of her scant Italian on her. When all her efforts succeeded in only drawing a blank look from the plump and happy woman, Jayme realised that she was not going to get very far in her quest to do something about her passport without the services of some English-speaking Italian.

With or without her passport, courtesy if nothing else decreed that she see her host again before she left, Jayme realised. So, since she was going to have to seek him out to thank him politely for all he had done for her, it seemed only logical that she bury her pride and ask for his assistance in the matter of her passport.

It had always been her belief that concerns of an unpleasant nature were best tackled first. That being so, Jayme left her chair and went to her bedroom door. At the door she paused for an instant, then straightened her shoulders and, hoping to appear as if she ached nowhere, opened the door.

A moment later she was going along a wide, white-painted, cool-looking hall, and discovering that the rooms of the villa appeared to be all on one level. Realising that she felt glad there were no stairs to go down, and that that meant she was not yet feeling a hundred per cent, she decided that she was the only one who was going to know it.

Passing an open door on her right, she looked in. It was a drawing-room, and although the man she was looking for was not in there, she was able to observe from the large and airy room that Nerone's villa was of quite some size.

She passed another couple of rooms before she eventually found Nerone in a smaller sized breakfast-room. Immediately he saw her, he was on his feet.

'Jayme!' he exclaimed, for all the word as though he had forgotten how, in fury, she had been *'signorina'* to him last night. The smile he had previously had for her seemed to have permanently disappeared, though, she noted. For there was not a glimmer of a smile on his good-looking features when, coming swiftly round to her, he promptly drew out a chair from the table. 'Please be seated,' he commanded sternly, 'and tell me what you're doing dressed and out of bed.'

'I'm leaving Italy today,' she began. 'That is ...'

'Out of the question!' he abruptly cut her off. 'I will not allow it!'

'You can't stop me!' Jayme flared, up in arms in a minute and wondering who did he think he was to... Swiftly she choked back more angry words as it dawned on her that this was no way to go about getting his help. Though what it was about this man that he could so easily provoke her to anger when up until last night her outbursts of temper had been more 'mild eruptions' than 'outbursts', she could not say. 'If I may begin again,' she swallowed her wrath to say more calmly, 'I'm hoping to leave Italy today, only I can't seem to find my passport.'

She thought he was about to say something, but all he did say before he moved away from her to go back to his seat at the opposite side of the breakfast table was, 'I see,' and Jayme saw that his expression was more bland than angry as, raising the coffee-pot, he enquired, 'Would you care for coffee? Rosa can soon bring another cup.'

'No, thank you,' she replied politely. She had more important things on her mind than to sit while Rosa was summoned and then sent to do her master's bidding. 'Actually, I was wondering—when you've had your breakfast, of course,' she inserted, endeavouring to remain polite, 'if you could help me contact the police. As you know, I don't speak Italian and...'

'Of course,' he said willingly—so willingly that Jayme could not but wonder if she had imagined that he had only minutes ago forcefully decreed that it was out of the question that she leave Italy that day. 'Now tell me exactly when you last had your passport.'

'I can remember having it in Verona—at the airport,' she obliged, 'but not after that.'

'Then we must telephone the police in Verona, at once,' Nerone decided. 'Come,' he added, and was on his feet again; that she must have her passport returned was much more important than his finishing his breakfast, it seemed. 'We will go to my study.'

Relief flooded through Jayme that he was taking such immediate action. She saw his eyes narrow, though, and heard what she was sure must be some kind of mild Italian swear word when, getting from her chair too quickly, she could not avoid her eyes reflecting the fact that her movement was painful.

'Hospital,' Nerone rapped grittily, 'would seem a better proposition than a journey to Verona, *signorina*!'

'I'm fine when I'm upright,' Jayme retorted. But she was glad that, whether she had angered him or not, he did not go striding to his study, but kept pace with her.

His study was a large, square, businesslike room. 'You will sit here, Jayme,' he directed, and purely, she knew, because she did not like to be bad friends with anyone, she began to feel more cheered that he had forgotten to be cross with her and was again calling her by her first name.

He went over to his desk and, after asking her full name, her date of birth and anything else he thought he might need to pass on, reached for his phone and was soon busy dialling.

Hope rose high in her when after a while Nerone started to make his enquiry. Shortly after that he spoke again, but in such a fast volley of Italian that the only words she could make out at all were English ones— her own name, in fact. Her hopes were still high when he finished his call, but when straight away he dialled another number, she had to wait for him to finish that call too before she could find out if her passport had been handed in.

'What did they say?' she demanded urgently.

'No one has reported finding your passport so far,' he came round to prop himself on the edge of his desk to tell her. 'I've been in touch with both the authorities in Verona and Torbole, and neither has any knowledge of your passport.'

'Oh, grief!' Jayme exclaimed, letting out a pent-up breath. 'Oh, how could I have been so careless...?'

'It could well be that someone with quick fingers took it from you without your being aware,' Nerone suggested. 'I imagine there could be quite a trade in passports for a certain criminal element in everyone's country.'

'But that could mean that I might never see it again!' she exclaimed.

'Not at all,' he said bracingly. 'The authorities in Verona told me that they are always having "mislaid" passports handed in. I feel sure that yours is only temporarily astray and will be handed in within a few days.'

'A few days!' Jayme repeated. 'But what am I going to do until then?' she spoke her thoughts out loud.

'Surely there is no great hurry for you to leave?' he questioned, and, when she had already reached the view that she had outstayed her welcome in his villa. 'You are not yet recovered from your accident,' he reminded her. 'Surely you can bear to allow me to make amends by staying in my home a little while longer?'

'I appreciate your offer,' Jayme told him in friendlier tones, 'but, apart from the fact that my mother will be expecting me home soon, I think it best that I leave.'

For long moments Nerone looked at her in the most disgruntled way. But, her decision made, Jayme concentrated hard not to wince as she stood up and prepared to leave his study.

Having stood up, though, she found she had brought herself that much nearer to a pair of brooding dark eyes. 'At the risk of offending you, *signorina*, might I suggest that you have more pride than sense?' he offered coldly.

It was not lost on Jayme that he knew quite well that their row last night had something to do with her leaving. But, while she realised this was the nearest he was going to come to making an apology—for, even if the reason they had rowed was still a trifle obscure to her, he had started it, not she—Jayme did have, as he suggested, quite a lot of pride.

'Grazie, signore,' she offered in return, and proudly she went back to her bedroom.

Having returned to her room, however, Jayme collapsed into the cream and gold chair and tried to ignore the fact that she did not feel too good. Instead she endeavoured to concentrate on what she must do now. The first essential, she supposed, must be to pack her clothes and, since it looked as if she was stuck in Italy for 'a few days' more, somehow find the tourist office and ask their help in finding the cheapest accommodation.

Pinning her hopes on her passport turning up very soon, Jayme eased herself out of her chair. She had just managed to put her empty suitcase on her bed prior to making a start on her packing, though, when she heard the Ferrari start up.

Why she should feel hurt that, quite clearly having better things to do than to hang around waiting for her to say her thank-yous and goodbyes, Nerone had gone out, she could not fathom. She tried to still an inner feeling of disquiet that she would not see him again, though she realised, of course, that she only felt disquieted because it didn't seem right to her that she should leave without first thanking him for his generous hospitality.

Packing her belongings, she found, was a tedious and tiring business. Rosa had unpacked for her in a quarter of the time, Jayme mused, and in a weak moment she knew she would not have made too many protests had Rosa come in and taken over for her.

But Rosa did not come in, and Jayme got over her weak moment and carried on with her packing. Then, more pulling than hefting, she manoeuvred her case down to the pale gold carpet. She was aware that it had taken an age for her to pack, and because her strength seemed, for the moment, to be used up, she went and sat down for a short while to recharge her batteries. Then, since she had not heard another outside sound since she had heard the Ferrari leave, she thought she had better go and find Rosa and thank her for all the services she had performed for her. At the same time, and since Jayme had no idea where exactly she was other than in some place either in or near Torbole, she would try and communicate to Rosa that she would like her to ring for a taxi.

The taxi fare, Jayme well knew as she left her room, was another expense she could quite well do without. But the thought of dragging not only herself but her suitcase to the tourist information office, when she had no idea where it was, seemed, even to her impecunious self, to make it a warranted expense.

To her surprise, however, Jayme could find the housekeeper nowhere. 'Rosa!' she called as, going along the wide hall, she opened doors on to a large dining-room, another large ante-room, and a vast kitchen, but all to no avail.

Realising that Rosa must have gone shopping, Jayme returned to her room and double-checked that she had left nothing behind, then she sat down to wait.

In all, she waited about three-quarters of an hour before she made up her mind that, wherever Rosa was, she hadn't just popped out to the shops for a few minutes. It was then that Jayme's pride gave her another nudge, and she began to feel that, although she had told Nerone of her intention to leave, the way that things were going she stood a chance of still being here when he got back.

She was not at all certain how she was going to find the tourist information office on her own, but, with the idea for some reason fixed in her head that Nerone had gone sailing but might soon be back, she took up her case and struggled with it out into the hall.

She had just reached the outside door when she heard the sound of a car approaching at speed. When the car stopped, she knew it was the Ferrari, and knew also that she had delayed her departure five minutes too long.

Her suitcase was down at her feet, and she was adjusting her thoughts to be certain that it was better this way anyway, and that really it was only polite to be able to thank Nerone, when, clearly in a hurry, he strode in through the door.

On seeing Jayme, however, he halted abruptly. She saw his glance go down to her case, then back to her face. And then, surprising her into realising that he wasn't in a hurry at all, she saw a hint of the smile she had thought she would never see again, and heard his voice, quite pleasant, as he said astonishingly, 'Ah, Jayme—have you had breakfast?'

'Breakfast?' she echoed, then found he had placed a gentle but firm hand beneath her elbow and was steering her towards the kitchen.

She later thought that the reason she went with him was perhaps because she had found his question so unexpected. Though what she had expected him to say, she was not sure about either. But whatever, she soon found herself seated in the vast kitchen, and came out of her surprise to find that Nerone, in between making some coffee, was serving her a doorstep wedge of bread, some butter, and some cheese.

'You see how helpless I am in the kitchen?' he enquired lightly—his way, she gathered, of apologising for the great piece of bread she would need a jaw like a hippopotamus to get her mouth around.

'I'm sure you're good at your regular profession,' Jayme murmured, 'but,' she went on, 'there's no need . . .'

'Ah, but there is,' he cut in solemnly, as he joined her at the table. 'Rosa was quite devastated when, on her way to her daughter's, she remembered that she had not served you breakfast this morning.'

'Oh, she shouldn't have worried,' Jayme told him earnestly, realising that this must be Rosa's day off and that Nerone had just come back from taking her to spend the day with her daughter. 'Rosa's been more than kind to me as it is. I should have liked to thank her before I left, though,' she went on. 'Could I ask you to pass on my grateful thanks?' she asked him.

'Of course,' he replied smoothly. 'Although I'm not too sure when exactly I will see her again.'

Jayme was again surprised. By then it was firmly fixed in her mind that Rosa would return that evening. But since Nerone, it seemed, was not being short-tempered about her decision to leave, Jayme felt able to ask him, quite pleasantly, 'Isn't this Rosa's day off?'

He shook his head, looking, she thought, rather fed up. 'For one day, or even two, I think perhaps I could manage. But,' he told her solemnly, 'Rosa received word this morning that her daughter, on whom she dotes, is ill. Nothing will do for her but that she must go to her straight away.' He was more solemn-eyed than ever as he tacked on, 'I've no idea at all when she will return.'

'Oh, I'm so sorry—about Rosa's daughter, I mean,' Jayme told him quickly.

'You are not at all sorry about my plight, eh?' he queried.

'Well, of course,' she told him hurriedly, realising that he seemed quite put out.

'Naturally, I told Rosa that she must take off what time she needs,' Nerone told her.

'Naturally,' Jayme smiled, and liked him that, even though he was put out, he had found it in him to tell Rosa that.

'But what am I to do meanwhile?' he asked.

'You?' she queried, not certain she knew what he meant.

'It is my vacation. A time I've looked forward to after night-and-day pressure that sometimes one has to live through in the business world,' he explained. 'But,' he continued, 'what rest is there for me when I—who as you've seen am useless in the kitchen—have to look after myself?'

It would have been comical, Jayme thought, had Nerone not been so serious. She realised, however, that some people could be absolutely brilliant in their chosen field, but could not otherwise so much as boil an egg when let loose in the kitchen. Quite obviously,

Nerone's forte lay in the business world. Clearly he was lost when it came to anything domestic.

'Can't you get another housekeeper?' she suggested, as she tried to be helpful. 'She need only be temporary until...'

'I don't want to spend the rest of my vacation in advertising and interviewing,' Nerone dismissed her suggestion out of hand. 'Impossible,' he said, and seemed about to say something more when suddenly he halted, and stared at her.

'What...?' Jayme queried, when it was plain that some new thought had just struck him.

'Of course,' he said, somewhat obscurely, 'that's it!'

'What's *it*?' she demanded, quite well aware that he spoke the most comprehensible English, but feeling she had lost him somewhere.

'Why didn't I think of it before?' he asked her.

'Think of what?' she asked, feeling more mystified than ever.

Nerone favoured her with a half-smile, and then, to her utter stupefaction, he announced, 'You shall look after me!'

'Me?' Jayme repeated incredulously, wincing as she made a jerky movement of surprise.

'I shouldn't want you to do too much,' Nerone told her quickly. 'Not until you are fully well again.'

'But I can't—t-take Rosa's p-place!' Jayme stammered.

'Why not?' he demanded, having made up his mind, apparently, and objecting strongly to the opposition she was putting up. 'Did you not tell me yourself that you helped your mother keep house?'

'*Helped*, yes,' she admitted.

'And that was for how many?' he questioned, but did not wait for her to reply, but went on. 'I am only one person for you to look after. Surely you can manage that?'

'Yes,' Jayme had to own. 'But that's not the point,' she protested.

'The point,' Nerone Mondadori said bluntly, clearly a man who did not care to have his will opposed, 'is that you are being deliberately stubborn.'

'No, I'm n...!'

'Yes, you are,' he silenced her. 'From the little you've told me, it's clear to me that you're here in my country without vast sums of money at your disposal. Yet here you are, knowing you cannot leave Italy until your passport is found—which, if you insist on leaving this villa, means you'll have to use your precious resources to pay for accommodation, when if you work for me your accommodation will cost you nothing and you will have a wage too...'

'I don't want your money!' Jayme erupted.

'You're being both stubborn *and* proud,' Nerone told her coldly, then went on sharply, 'Come now, Jayme, can you not see that you would be better living and working here for the next two or three weeks than...'

'Two or three weeks?' she butted in, totally amazed.

'In two or three weeks Rosa should have returned, and by then your passport is bound to have been handed in to the police,' Nerone told her.

The thought of it being two or three weeks before her passport came to light was one of nightmarish proportions to Jayme. No way could she afford to stay in Italy for that length of time. Swiftly a following thought struck her that she could afford to stay if she accepted Nerone's offer—but hurriedly she pushed that thought away.

'But I don't want Rosa's job! I already have a job. My employer will be expecting me back at my desk on Monday at the latest,' she told him quickly, as though to deny her previous weakening thought.

'Without a passport you'll be going nowhere!' Nerone told her toughly.

Jayme tossed him an unfriendly look. He was a man, it was becoming plainer by the second, who would brook no opposition to an idea once born. 'My mother's expecting me home too!' she told him snappily.

'There's no problem there, surely,' he returned brusquely. 'It will take only minutes for you to telephone her about your altered plans.'

'It's not as easy as that,' Jayme persisted in arguing, barely realising that, from positively asserting that she would not stay on, she was now giving him excuses for why she must go home. 'My mother thinks I'm still unofficially engaged to Tusco Bianco, and I don't want to tell her that I'm not until I'm back home,' she told him.

'Then if you have to,' Nerone said sourly, 'tell her that you're staying on for a few weeks to be near to him!'

'I can't lie to her!' Jayme exclaimed, but found her outrage ridden straight over.

'By omission,' he snarled, 'you already have!'

You utter swine! Jayme silently fumed, not liking his home truths one little bit—for all her 'omissions' had been to spare her mother worry. 'I can't cook Italian style!' she told him belligerently.

'I'd be surprised if you could,' Nerone retorted. Then, as if he considered the matter settled, 'Eat your bread and cheese,' he commanded. 'I'll take your case back to your room.'

Jayme glared at his departing back. Somehow, whether she wanted it or not, it seemed that she had just got herself a job as a temporary housekeeper!

CHAPTER FOUR

A WEEK later Jayme realised that she had come to terms with what, last Thursday, had seemed to be slipping out of her control. By the following Wednesday she had long since reached the conclusion that, since she would be beholden to no one, to work for Nerone would be a way of repaying him. Not only for his kindness in taking her in, but for his hospitality—when that accident had been her fault entirely, with no blame attached to him. She had by that time ceased asking him daily to check to see if her passport had been handed in—he had said he would let her know the moment he heard anything. By that Wednesday evening, as she lay in her bed, she discovered that not only had she adjusted to being housekeeper to Signor Nerone Mondadori di Vallanetto, but also—to her confusion—she did not feel anywhere as near as unhappy as she had!

She still felt, though, that she had made a big fool of herself in coming to Italy to see Tusco Bianco. Nor was she yet over the humiliating feeling that she had been a pushover for his lies. She was therefore determined that never again was she going to be taken in by a man's lies. Never again would she be a gullible pushover. She'd see the lies coming the next time, she vowed, and be ready for them.

Her thoughts drifted for a while, and the next she knew was that Nerone Mondadori was in her head. And what about him? What a mixture of a man he was! He had assured her that he was helpless in the kitchen, and to a certain extent that was true, for, unless the meal came out of a packet or a tin, they would have starved in the first days of her being engaged as his temporary housekeeper. Because, for all his stated need of someone to look after him, it had been he who had looked after *her*, initially!

'You go and sit out on the terrace and let the healing sun get on you,' he had instructed her when he had come across her searching through the kitchen cupboards for something for lunch that first day of her starting her new duties.

'But . . .' she had tried to argue.

'When you are well, you'll remember today with some wonder,' Nerone cut her off, and made it sound as though he would work her so hard when she was fully recovered that she would wish she had given in to him that day.

'If you insist,' she had given in, and, hoping to hide from him the fact that she felt as though she had more tender places than *un*tender places, she creaked her way out on to the terrace and into the warm sun— and was straight away lost in awe of the view.

In all, three days were to go by before Jayme was allowed to hold so much as a duster in her hands. 'You're certain you're feeling well enough to begin your duties?' Nerone enquired sternly in the kitchen on Sunday morning as he ordered her to sit down and she refused.

'I shall die of boredom if I don't do something,' she had told him—more in crossness than in truth.

Nerone gave her a thorough scrutiny, and seemed to be satisfied that she looked fit enough to wait on him. 'Very well,' he agreed, and told her loftily, 'You can cook English bacon and eggs for me.'

'If you'd like to go to the breakfast-room—' she suggested.

'We'll eat breakfast in here,' he countermanded her suggestion.

Jayme was aware of his eyes on her as she busied herself setting the table and cooking the bacon and eggs which she surmised he had purchased along with some other fresh food yesterday. Though when she flicked a glance at him, it was to see that his eyes were elsewhere, and that he seemed deep in thought and unaware of her presence.

Having insisted that she sit at the breakfast-table, however, it was as she sat munching on toast that he suddenly came away from his own thoughts and queried abruptly, 'Have you telephoned your mother yet?'

The fact that she had not yet telephoned her mother again was a source of some anxiety to Jayme. 'Not yet,' she told him, 'but I shall have to do it today.'

'Have you decided what you're going to tell her?' he asked.

Jayme shook her head. 'She'll worry if I tell her about the accident, she'll worry if I tell her I've lost my passport—and I just can't tell her about Tusco,' she said unhappily.

'You have a problem, *signorina*,' Nerone commented coolly, and got up, and with the prompt, 'She's going to worry anyway if she doesn't hear from you soon,' he left her to worry some more about making that call.

In the end, when Jayme did put a call through to England, it was her mother who made it easier for her. Using the phone that was still in her bedroom, Jayme told her mother that she had decided to extend her stay for a couple of weeks.

'Why, that's lovely, darling!' her mother had exclaimed warmly. 'You're way overdue for a holiday—and what better place than Italy?' she'd teased. She had then gone on to offer to ring Jayme's employer and tactfully break the news to him that he would be without the services of his secretary for a couple more weeks.

Jayme could not help but be amazed, though, at the way her mother had so easily accepted the idea that she could so uncaringly take further time off work. Surely she must know that it was not in her nature to let anyone down—and that included her employer?

It was only a little while later, however, that she realised that, having loved deeply herself, her mother would consider that where love was involved there was little that one would not do, be it against one's nature or not.

Which, Jayme puzzled, gave her food for thought that she, loving Tusco, should find it impossible to go against her nature, and prove her love to him in the way he wanted.

But she forgot Tusco for a while when, glancing at the phone she had just put down, she suddenly wondered why, when Rosa had received word that her daughter needed her, she had not heard the telephone ring. She shrugged the stray thought away, though, as she recalled that Nerone had never said that word had come via the telephone. In any case, with every mechanical or electronic piece of equipment in the villa being of the most up-to-date kind, it could quite well be that the telephone system was such that the phone Nerone had plugged into her room had its own individual line.

Jayme started thinking of Nerone again, and her thoughts stayed with him for a while. He was at times brusque—to the point of rudeness—while at others he could be charm itself.

'May I know where your room is, Nerone, so that I can clean and make your bed?' she had asked him on Monday.

'No, you may not!' he replied curtly, and she realised it had nothing to do with the fact that he did not think she was up to anything of too strenuous a nature yet, when he added shortly, 'I can make my own bed.'

'Suit yourself!' she had flared, only to witness his charm when he had returned,

'I should not like you to think that I'm completely helpless,' and suddenly he was smiling.

'As if I would!' she'd replied tartly and, she had to own, a shade cheekily. She had thought then that he'd seemed on the verge of breaking out into laughter, but, as his velvety eyes humorously met hers, he suddenly glanced down at her all at once upward-curving mouth and stilled, then scowled. Then, confusing her still more, he strode quickly from the room.

Her thoughts grasshoppered back, as sleep tried to claim her, to how she had come in for some of his wrath on Sunday, too. She snuggled down in her bed and recalled that while Nerone had been doing the catering they had eaten either in the kitchen or outside on the terrace. But now that she had taken over, and certain that Rosa must eat her meals in her own apartment, she had laid the table in the dining-room that lunchtime, and had laid it for one only. It was not long, however, before she was to hear that such an arrangement did not find favour with the master of the house.

She saw his eyes rake over her slender form as, expecting to see him seated, she entered the dining-room with his soup starter. But he was not seated, and stood eyeing her grimly as she placed the soup tureen on the table. He made no attempt to sit down, though, and as Jayme glanced questioningly at him, he demanded grittily, 'Are you on some idiotic "no lunch" diet?'

'No,' she replied, 'I've never dieted in my...'

'Where, then,' he cut in toughly, 'are you intending to eat?'

'In the kitchen,' she replied, and was astonished, to say the least, when he caught hold of her, at the same time pulling his chair out from the table. He was certainly a man of action! In the next moment Jayme found that she was seated in his place, and that Nerone had gone striding to the kitchen.

She was still striving to get her breath back when a few moments later he returned, carrying her place setting. 'You will be good enough to take your meals with me!' he told her sharply.

'But it isn't right!' she protested.

'You are a snob?' he questioned.

'No!' she asserted. 'What I am is your temporary housekeeper,' she went on hotly, and, gathering a full head of steam, 'Rosa is your permanent housekeeper, but I feel sure she doesn't eat her meals with you.'

'You, as you say, are her temporary replacement,' Nerone replied sharply, never at a loss for words, she was discovering—in any language—'but you are also a guest in my country.'

'But...'

'You will permit me, *signorina*,' he told her stiffly, 'to afford you every Italian courtesy.' The matter was closed as far as he was concerned, Jayme realised when, reaching for the soup tureen, he ordered, 'Pass your soup dish.'

Jayme did so, but did not care very much for the way he was bossing her around. 'What about when you entertain?' she drew out of some perverseness in her nature. 'Will you still want to afford me every Italian courtesy on the occasions you entertain?' she enquired, and received a menacing look for her trouble.

'I will let you know,' he clipped, and for the rest of the meal showed his Italian courtesy by for the most part ignoring her.

Oddly, though, having been the one to mention that he might want to entertain, Jayme discovered that who he might want to entertain occupied more of her thoughts than the fact that sometimes, without too much effort, Nerone could look thoroughly irritated by her. No doubt his 'entertaining' would be in the size and shape of some beautiful dark-eyed, dark-haired Italian female, she mused, as she unconsciously played with her own platinum-blonde locks. Not that it bothered her, she shrugged. As soon as her passport came to light she would be off.

Well, qualified her conscience just before sleep claimed her, after Nerone's goodness in giving her shelter, perhaps she would stay until Rosa returned. Or, failing that, spend some time in home-baking so she could stock up his freezer before she left.

Jayme awoke early on Thursday morning, and left her bed to go swinging into her bathroom, overjoyed to be feeling as good as new and with not so much as an ache or pain in sight. She had a quick bath and, having dressed in a light summer dress, went, as was now her habit, through the french doors of her room out on to the terrace.

The spot where Nerone had had his villa built was absolutely idyllic, she thought, not for the first time. Set high on a plateau of land, the villa was hidden from the road by tall cypress trees, yet at the same time had a clear view of a part of the lake. Blue skies were mirrored in the clear waters. Lush vegetation rolled down to the shore. Here and there were scattered the orangey-red pantiled roofs of other villas, and the view, and the serene silence, was magical. There too, in mammoth splendour, was the gigantic mountain of limestone rock that appeared to Jayme to have dropped from the sky straight into the middle of this part of Lake Garda.

It was the same monolithic rock she had seen from her seat by the lakeside at Torbole, Jayme had realised, though it was true to say that the magnificent towering mountains of rock and vegetation appeared to surround that north-eastern end of the lake.

'You're enjoying the view?' Unbeknown to her, Nerone had joined her.

Startled that she had not heard him, though she guessed that her utter captivation by the scenery might have something to do with that, Jayme nevertheless smiled.

'I don't think I should ever tire of it if I lived here for ever and ever,' she told him, wanting just one more minute of "her" view, before she went to prepare breakfast.

She caught a glimpse of his pleased smile as she turned again to contemplate the scenery. 'How are you feeling today?' he asked, though she was aware by then that he took more notice of what his eyes told him than of her declaration that she felt 'fine'.

'Great,' she told him, and heard a smile in his voice when he replied drily,

'Today I think I can believe you.'

Jayme laughed lightly and went indoors. Suddenly she was feeling as though there was not one single cloud on her horizon.

It did not last, and, she realised, she had only herself to blame. She and Nerone breakfasted on bread—cut thinly by her—cheese and ham, with strong black coffee, which Nerone made. They were just finishing their coffee when he told her that he was going sailing at Riva del Garda a short distance away. 'Would you care to come with me?' he asked casually.

'No!' she answered him sharply before she had given herself time to think. 'Er—thank you, but no,' she added more politely.

'You're afraid of the water?' he questioned, his friendly tone already starting to fade.

'I . . . no,' she had to tell him honestly, and later heard him drive off without so much as an *arrivederci*.

Jayme got on with a few domestic tasks with her earlier feeling of wellbeing gone. She felt totally out of sorts and, asking herself why she had refused Nerone's offer to take her sailing, she realised with a prickle of unease that, while it was true that she was unafraid of the water, she was afraid of something.

It was something of a puzzle to her to discover of what she was afraid. But, never one not to face facts, she put her mind to finding out just what she was afraid of, that she should refuse an outing which she knew full well she would enjoy.

Some few minutes later she was reeling from realising that, having so recently been hurt by Tusco Bianco, her self-protective instincts had rallied round to defend her and to do what they could to ensure that she was not hurt again.

Which, she realised another few minutes later, was totally ridiculous. Because there had been no ulterior motive in Nerone's casual offer to take her sailing. Quite plainly he had only asked her on the impulse of the moment. For heaven's sake, she had a feeling sometimes that he could barely tolerate her, so it was for sure that he hadn't any 'designs on her virtue'!

Thoroughly fed up with herself suddenly, Jayme spent the next hour in working hard at her chores as if in the hope that she would work herself into a better frame of mind.

When an hour later she felt no better, and realising that since Nerone had gone sailing she might not see him again before dark, she decided that what might be needed was a breath of air outside the villa.

Intending to go only a short way, Jayme secured the villa and put the key in the skirt pocket of her dress. There was quite a long drive to walk down before she reached the hilly road, she discovered, but, having made it to the end of the drive, she turned right and headed off down the hill.

Her thoughts were still on the way her fear of being hurt again had seen her deprive herself of the pleasure of a day's sailing as she descended the hill on the tarmacked but pavementless road. Feeling glum, she fully recognised that Nerone obviously didn't give two hoots whether she went sailing with him or not. Her sharp 'No!' of refusal had not only killed any suggestion of friendly feeling in him towards her, but had also established that the Lago di Garda would freeze over before he would offer her the chance to go anywhere with him again.

Sighing without being certain just why she was sighing, Jayme halted near a high wall as a car came hurtling by. Once the car had gone by, however, she walked on a couple of yards and then saw a gate in the wall. Closer inspection revealed that there was a handwritten notice attached to the gate which appeared to be informing anyone interested of the opening and closing times. The only English on the handwritten sign, however, stated quite clearly, 'No Camping'.

Delighted to realise that she must have come across a public park, Jayme observed that to the left of the gate towards the top of the wall was an official-looking sign. Moving over to it, she saw that the sign appeared to have been put there by the Nago-Torbole council, and had a message stamped out in five different languages. The English language one read 'Public Olive Grove'. In the next second Jayme was back at the brown-painted gate. A second later she was inside the public olive grove—and peace washed over her.

Never had she known such a tranquil place. It was not a large olive grove, but large enough to house a considerable number of wooden benches scattered about where one could take one's ease.

She wandered around the grove, that was grassed and had, besides olive trees, many other trees and shrubs as well. She strolled over to a tree which she was sure had elderberries growing on it, but which, on closer inspection, turned out to be some other sort of tree. She next strolled over to a part of the grove where what seemed to be a fishpond or paddling pool had been constructed, but about which, since there was neither water nor fish there, she could not make a more accurate guess.

It did not take her many minutes to stroll round the entire olive grove. But, having done so, it was then that she made a discovery which she found warming.

For as she settled herself down on one of the wooden benches with the intention of breathing in the serenity of the place, suddenly a nearby clock chimed the quarter hour. Almost simultaneously, a beautiful smell wafted into her nostrils. It was the smell of wild mint.

Jayme knew, at that instant, that she had been in this place before. This, she knew without question, was the place Nerone had brought her to that day she had walked in front of his car.

Her thoughts flitted on and around Nerone and his kindness to her that day. She was now aware that he was a man who liked his privacy, and on that basis alone could have quite easily—and with a clear conscience, since the accident was entirely her fault—left her where she was. Or, if that was perhaps not the kind of thing a man of his calibre would do, he could have called an ambulance, or even dropped her off at the nearest hospital.

Jayme's thoughts and feelings for Nerone were warm when, an hour later, she retraced her steps back to the villa. Had she been able to cook Italian style then she would, with gratitude in her heart that he had not just dumped her but had taken her into his home, have made him the best Italian dinner she could think of.

As it was, she had her head filled with wondering what she could cook for him which he might enjoy when, as she walked up the drive and then inserted the key into the door lock of the villa, suddenly the door opened and, shaken, she saw Nerone standing there looking little short of murderous.

'Where the hell have you been?' he demanded furiously.

Oh, help, thought Jayme, realising that not only had she been wrong in thinking she would not see him until it was too dark for him to sail any more but that seemingly he objected to his housekeeper, albeit temporary, taking time off without his permission.

'So I'll get your lunch,' she replied coolly and, refusing to be intimidated, put her nose in the air and went airily past him.

She did not get very far, though, because before she could make it along the hall and to the kitchen Nerone had come after her. In a flash one of his hands had snaked out and was clamped around her upper arm as he spun her around to face him.

Jayme's heart quailed to see that he looked more murderous than ever, but, while she strongly resented being manhandled in this way, she could also see that there would be one almighty explosion if she got angry too.

'To hell with lunch!' he roared, clearly incensed, his anger, it seemed, having nothing to do with his being hungry. 'Where have you been?' he demanded again.

'Only down to...'

An irate Italian expletive rent the air. 'To Torbole,' he crashed through what she had been about to say, and, his manner thunderously accusing, 'You've been to Torbole looking for your ex-fiancé!' he raged.

'I've what?' Jayme challenged, and as the import of what he had just said fully smote her, she too grew incensed and, with her pride all at once in an uproar, she forgot entirely any notion that she must not get angry. 'What the *hell* do you think I am?' she yelled, veritable sparks flashing from her sea-green eyes as she glared at him.

Hostilely Nerone looked blackly at her, then, even while he frowned into her sparking eyes, a change seemed to come over him. As his eyes studied the rest of her face, suddenly, and to her astoundment, he positively hurled her arm from him and went striding away down the hall.

Feeling more than a little shaken, Jayme followed him with her eyes, then went marching stormily to her room.

Once she was away from him, however, her temper rapidly cooled. But she was no nearer to fathoming his Italian temperament when twenty minutes later she decided that, since he did not appear to be too hungry, he could wait for his lunch.

Just to show, though, that she was never going to be able to fathom this aristocratic Italian, there suddenly came a tap at her door. Then, after she had set her face in a polite but cool mask and went to answer it, she discovered that the lofty aristocrat had some quite estimable qualities. For, although his expression was grave, it was with some charm that he spoke as, holding her eyes with his own, he began, 'I should like to apologise for causing you offence, *signorina*. I already knew of your pride, which only makes it more wrong that I should accuse you of chasing after any man the way I accused you. My only excuse,' he went on, when so far Jayme had not said a word, 'is that I was angry that, when you had seemed so well this morning, you must have walked down into Torbole, which would mean a fatiguing climb back, and all before you are fit to tackle such a climb.'

'I didn't go as far as Torbole,' Jayme murmured, and saw a hint of a smile touch Nerone's attractive mouth.

'Are you going to forgive me, and come and help me eat the lunch I've prepared?' he asked.

What could she do? His charm was a potent force. And that—when he was by his own admission useless

in the kitchen—made the fact that he had endeavoured to prepare a meal add up to a most handsome
apology.

'Of course,' Jayme told him simply, and went with
him to the kitchen where he had prepared a cold meat
and salad lunch, with fresh fruit to follow.

Any lingering sign of strain between them disappeared over lunch. So much so that when only a short
while ago Jayme had decided he could go hang before
she would tell him where she had been that morning,
suddenly she found she was telling him all about her
discovery of the public olive grove.

'It's quite an enchanting place, and there's such a
feeling of tranquillity there,' she told him.

'I think you have fallen a little in love with this
place, Jayme,' Nerone teased her, and because,
without really knowing it, she felt happy again, Jayme
laughed lightly.

'I think you may be right,' she smiled, and, as her
eyes went dreamy, 'There wasn't a soul there while I
was there, and...' she broke off. 'Oh, how can I describe the feel of the place? It's...' again she broke
off, and then, 'But I forget, you already know the
place. It was where you took me that day of the
accident!'

'You remembered it?' he asked, perhaps remembering that she had been more semi-conscious than
awake that day.

Jayme shook her head. 'Not the place so much as
the smell of wild mint, and a church clock striking
somewhere.'

'Ah,' Nerone murmured. 'The first words I heard
from you to let me know you were of this world were
"I can smell mint".'

Jayme smiled, and after that they spoke of other
things—though it seemed to her that what they spoke
of mainly was her. First he asked more about her work
apart from helping her mother. Then he asked about
her sisters and their ages, and whether Leonie was
still a timid, nervous child, or had grown out of it.
And all in all, Jayme found Nerone so easy to get on
with that she could barely believe that so short a time
ago he had made her so irate that she could, without
any further pushing, have physically hit him.

After lunch, when she declined to use the dishwasher for so few dishes, he insisted on helping her
with the washing-up, and even laughed out loud his
very masculine and pleasant-sounding laugh when she
could not hold back the comment, 'When you apologise, you really apologise!'

'You ain't seen nothing yet!' rolled off his tongue,
and it sounded so funny coming from his Italian lips
that Jayme simply broke up.

She recovered to see his glance go from the mer-
riment in her eyes to the laughter curving her mouth.
Then Nerone insisted that she should rest until four
o'clock when, because needs must, he would take her
shopping for provisions.

'I ought to go on my own,' Jayme donned her temporary housekeeper hat to suggest.

'When you've fully recovered your strength,' he replied firmly, and even though she tried to assure him
that she felt she had already fully recovered her
strength, he still insisted that he would take her
shopping.

Which, as the clock struck four, he did. Jayme
found pleasure in sitting in the Ferrari beside him as
he headed it down into Torbole. She could not help
a glance at the public olive grove as they passed

though, and when her glance came away her eyes met those of Nerone, and in mutual harmony they both smiled.

Their shopping jaunt was a success. Jayme enjoyed the outing, and she rather had a feeling that Nerone had not found it too irksome either.

Thursday gave way to Friday, and Friday to Saturday and Sunday, and then the weekend was over. Oddly, however, when Jayme would have thought that Nerone might have decided on any one of those days to indulge himself in the sport of sailing, he did not do so, but seemed to prefer to stay around the villa.

She got out of bed on Monday morning and smiled quietly to herself at the thought that not another cross word had passed between them since that flare-up last Thursday. Everything seemed to augur well for the remainder of her housekeeping stint to be completed in perfect harmony, Jayme thought serenely as she bathed and dressed and then went along to the kitchen.

Nerone was there before her and was drinking a cup of coffee while he read the morning paper. 'Good morning, Jayme,' he looked up to greet her pleasantly.

'*Buon giorno*, Nerone,' she replied with a smile, and set to to slice some bread.

They breakfasted together, as was now usual, and conversed easily as was now their custom, the meal consisting mainly of bread, cheese and ham.

'We're running a little short of fresh fruit,' Jayme commented, after a minute or so of companionable silence.

'We'll go to Torbole after breakfast,' Nerone replied. 'It...'

'Actually,' she interrupted him, an earnest look on her face, 'I think I'm quite strong enough now to go and do some shopping on my own.'

For some seconds it seemed to her that Nerone was about to object most emphatically. Then, as he looked at the seriousness of her unblinking expression, he appeared to change his mind. He enquired quietly, 'A matter of honour, is it, Jayme?'

Silently she nodded. 'Sort of,' she told him, and was pleased when, after studying her for a few more seconds, he said,

'Very well.' She was not so very pleased, however, when just before she got up from the table, Nerone pulled out his wallet, extracted a fistful of lire and passed them over to her.

'What's this?' she questioned, eyeing it warily.

'Do you suppose you'll be able to purchase fruit without money?' he queried teasingly.

'I have money,' Jayme told him sharply, and quickly saw that he did not like some of her comments either.

'I trust you've no real wish to offend by suggesting you pay my household expenses out of your own purse,' he uttered stiffly.

'Good grief, it's only a little fruit I intend to...'

'Enough!' Nerone chopped her off. 'I'm allowing you your honour, *signorina*, kindly allow me mine!'

Jayme drew a startled breath. Looking at it that way, she could see that she was in real danger of causing grave offence. So, suddenly, she smiled. 'Well, if you put it like that,' she murmured.

Stonily, Nerone stared at her for some seconds, and then suddenly his cold expression started to thaw. His grin, when it came, was, Jayme thought, wonderful to see. And all was 'all friends' between them again when he told her, 'You are, without doubt, a most aggravating creature!'

An hour later Jayme set off to do her little bit of shopping. There was a breeze blowing as she stepped from the drive and on to the road, but, dressed in cotton slacks and her long-sleeved cotton sweater, she felt warm enough.

In no time she was walking by the public olive grove which she had discovered for herself the previous Thursday and, as it seemed unthinkable that she should walk on by, she popped in for a few minutes, recaptured the magic she had found there on Thursday, then left, thinking to herself that it would be a splendid place to break her uphill climb on the return journey.

Once she was on the road outside again, it did not take her many minutes before she had reached the part she had trodden when she had hurried away from Torbole nearly two weeks ago.

She had been quite distraught then, she remembered, so it was hardly surprising to her that she barely recognised the road she was now walking. What did surprise her was the fact that, with the road being so steeply hilly, and bearing in mind that she had been toting her large suitcase at the time, she had been able to hurry at all!

When Jayme reached the bottom of the hill she took a right fork away from the shores of the lake. She wanted to be happy, she didn't want to be reminded of Tusco Bianco and the spot where she had seen him embracing his new love.

Making her way past shops with gaily coloured headsquares hung up in profusion outside, Jayme discovered that her lack of Italian was no barrier when it came to her buying the fruit she required.

From there she went and selected several picture postcards, then decided to go and have a cup of coffee in one of the street cafés while she thought what she would write to her mother and her sisters.

It crossed her mind as she sat in the sun, ordered her coffee and penned an uncomplicated few words to Leonie, that she could well be back in England before her cards reached home. As yet there was no word from Rosa, so how much longer she was going to be away, Jayme had no idea. But surely, if her passport was going to turn up, it would have done so by now.

But whatever... Suddenly all thought in Jayme's head ceased. *'Jayme!'* a voice she knew from a couple of months back cried.

She looked up, saw Tusco Bianco, and realised, far too late, that while there must have been a five per cent chance that she would bump into him in Torbole, she had nothing prepared to say to him, and knew not whether she should cut him or acknowledge him.

'Tusco!' She found her inner self had made up her mind for her. Then, as for having nothing prepared to say to him, she discovered that her pride, when pushed, gave her brilliant powers of invention. 'Join me for coffee,' she invited, and, because whatever Tusco was he wasn't slow-witted, so he must know that she just didn't 'happen' to be in Torbole, but must have come there looking for him, she confessed, 'I've come especially to see you.'

'How—er—nice of you,' he said warily, but for all his wariness he took the chair next to her, and Jayme had a few moments in which to marshal her thoughts when a waiter came and took his order for a *cappuccino*.

Fortunately, she hurriedly recapped, her letters to him, though affectionate, had not been of the smoochy variety. Added to that was the fact that, with Tusco hopping from lodging to lodging the way he had, it could be that quite a few of the letters she had written had not reached him.

'I know this isn't a very private place to tell you what I have to,' Jayme began quietly, though with the tourist season tailing off there were few customers outside the street café, 'but I felt, since I'd given you my solemn promise to marry you, that I should come in person to tell you that I've changed my mind.'

'You've changed your mind!' Tusco exclaimed, and, looking at him and seeing how he was having a hard time trying to look as though the bottom had just dropped out of his world, Jayme noticed for the first time what a very weak chin he had.

'I'm sorry,' she apologised. As he was doing his level best to look as though she had just dealt him a mortifying blow, she tried to look as though it hurt her to have to tell him what she had to. 'I made a mistake,' she went on. 'I didn't realise it at first,' she added, to cover any of the letters that had got through. 'But after a while, I realised...' Her voice faded. Suddenly she became aware that by labouring the point she was in danger of going over the top.

'You realised that marriage between us was not what you wanted?' he asked, and Jayme nodded, and, when he gave an exaggerated sigh she just knew, right there and then, what a sham he was. There was no sub-stance to the man; he was acting, as he would always act a part. She knew then that when they went their separate ways he would forget her—as had been shown in the past—and would take up a fresh acting role with whoever he happened to be with next.

But, having saved her face by finding that she wasn't backward in the Thespian department when pushed, Jayme extended her right hand to him, intending to give him a 'no hard feelings, I hope' handshake of farewell.

She supposed though that, having belatedly got Tusco's measure, she was not all that surprised when, instead of shaking her hand, he caught hold of it in a warm, intimate hold. Then, forgetful apparently that he had not sent one single solitary word of communication to her in going on for three months, 'But I cannot let you go, my darling,' he whispered soulfully, his eyes moist. 'You must let me...'

What she must 'let him' Jayme never got to hear. For just then, and to make them both jump, another voice cut in harshly, 'Is this man bothering you?'

At the sound of the authoritarian voice, Tusco abruptly let go of her hand, and Jayme forgot him as, startled, she looked up to see a tall and aristocratic Italian. 'Nerone!' she exclaimed, her heart starting to race. But even as she recognised that he was absolutely furious about something, she remembered his question. 'N-no,' she stammered, 'Tusco's n-not troubling me. We—er—knew each other in England.'

'Ah,' murmured Nerone, and seemed to her to rock back on his heels a little as his glance went to study Tusco. 'Then perhaps, *cara,*' he said deliberately, 'you should introduce us.' And while Jayme went dumbstruck to realise that Nerone had just intimately called her 'dear', she went from being dumbstruck to being utterly amazed when he waited no longer for her to perform the introductions but took over from her to tell Tusco, 'I am Nerone Mondadori di Vallanetto—Jayme's betrothed,' and, while she stared openmouthed, 'You must be Tusco Bianco, who was privileged to be a house guest in my fiancée's home for a short while.' Jayme closed her mouth, but she was still in shock when Nerone bade her, 'Come, my heart,' and, taking some notes from his wallet, put them down on the table to pay for her coffee, then told her, 'I think seeing your ex-house guest must have made you forget that we have an appointment in five minutes.'

With that, he put a hand on her arm and, as she automatically moved and he helped her to her feet, pushed her bag at her. Then, without another word to Tusco, he steered her towards his car.

They were in the Ferrari and were heading up the winding road to the villa when Jayme got her breath back and began to fume. How dared he—the high-handed devil! Who did he think he was?

Nerone had drawn his car up outside the villa before she got the chance to ask him. He was furious, she knew that, as with his hand again on her arm he guided her straight to the sitting-room. But by then, if he was furious, then so too was she.

'Have you gone stark, staring mad?' She turned to face him the moment he let go of her arm.

'Have you no pride at all?' Nerone hurled at her.

'*Pride?*' Jayme exploded.

'*Si*, pride! Are you so weak that...'

'I was handling the situation extremely well until you came and...'

'It looked like it!' Nerone roared. 'From holding hands, he'd have had you in some hotel bedroom in two minutes if I hadn't come along and...'

The crisp sound of her hand coming into sharp and violent contact with the side of his face made Jayme aware that she had hit him. She was unrepentant, though, and she stood her ground. That was, she thought she was unrepentant, but that was before her eyes left the side of his face where her hand had landed, and she saw the demoniacal light that had come into his eyes.

Clearly no female had ever lashed out at him so before, and Nerone, having growled something in Italian which didn't sound too complimentary, took a menacing step forward. 'No!' she cried.

She tried to back away, but he was quicker as, taking another stride forward, he grabbed hold of her wrists. 'You will pay!' he snarled, and Jayme knew then, as his hands went from her wrists and his arms came around her, that pay she would, and that Nerone would demand full retribution for the insult of that slap.

Strangely, though, although his mouth met hers fiercely at first, that fierceness did not last. She was still struggling in his hold when suddenly the iron bands of his arms that bound her to him eased their pressure, and gently, or so it seemed to her, his lips began to give, not take, as he teased her lips apart.

What was more shattering to Jayme, though, was her sudden inability, in the face of such gentleness, to fight him. Shaken, she ceased struggling. And, barely aware what she was doing, she held on to him.

When his mouth left hers and he looked tenderly down at her, all her will to oppose him seemed to vanish. So that, when next his lips claimed hers, she melted against him and, without any known volition, gave him her lips.

Time stood still for a little while then as they embraced. Nerone trailed kisses from her mouth down her throat and aroused such sensations in her that she clutched on to him for support.

Gently then he moved her to a long couch in the room, and they lay down on it. Nerone was partly lying over her when she felt his hand come beneath her sweater. 'Oh!' she murmured when he captured her breast. And that was when reality began to return.

For, whether Nerone thought her 'Oh!' was an 'Oh!' of protest, or what he thought, she was too lost to comprehend. She was too shy, too, to tell him that her 'Oh!' had been as much a pleased sound of wanting as anything else. But suddenly Nerone was pulling back from her.

'Jayme—Jayme,' he murmured hoarsely as he looked into her bewildered eyes. Then, while she grew more bewildered to know what that meant—if anything at all—he made her more bewildered still by moving from her, and from the couch—and by going swiftly from the room!

CHAPTER FIVE

FOR how many seconds Jayme stared at the door after Nerone had gone, she had no idea. But all at once she was galvanised into action, and went hastily to her bedroom and closed the door.

Good heavens, had that been her on that couch with Nerone? Feeling stunned, she could hardly believe that any man could so quickly arouse such emotions in her that she was well on the way to forgetting everything!

Her face flamed with colour as the thought winged in that when Nerone had pulled away from her she had been lost to everything but the sensations he had created in her. Oh, grief, she thought, winded, what would have happened had he not pulled back from her? Would she have...

Just as Jayme was unable to finish that question, she was unable to supply the answer. She knew enough about herself, however, to know that there was no way she could experience the emotions she had felt while she had been in Nerone's arms if she was in love with someone else. Which therefore made it very plain to her that she did not love Tusco Bianco as much as she had thought she did. How could she, and still behave, and feel, and—and yes—want another man the way she had?

She was still feeling shaky inside half an hour later. Some of her confusion had cleared, however, and she had gone from wondering about this new person inside her which Nerone Mondadori had brought to life, to wondering—what about him? It was true, she supposed, that one just didn't go around physically lashing out at men of his calibre and expect to get off scot free. But surely, the way things had been heading between the two of them, it had gone past being a matter of retribution.

Jayme was not quite sure how she felt when, some minutes later, she realised that though Nerone had quite plainly desired her, something—maybe something naïve in her response—had put him off. Another few moments later and she was never more glad that, whatever construction he had placed on her murmured 'Oh!', his desire for her had not been to the exclusion of all else.

A second half-hour passed during which she realised that she was going to have to face seeing Nerone again, but that she would very much prefer not to have to do so.

When ultimately she gathered up her courage and left her bedroom, she had come to several very definite conclusions. For one, Nerone could start looking after himself—she was leaving. For another, that afternoon would see her presenting herself at the tourist information office in Torbole asking for their help in finding her inexpensive accommodation—as had been her plan to start with. First, though, since it seemed certain by now that her passport was not going to turn up, she would have to discover where the nearest British Consulate was. Belatedly it had occurred to her that perhaps she should have contacted them before now.

Having therefore decided that she would seek Nerone out to tell him of her decision to leave, Jayme went to the drawing-room. He was not there. Next she went to the kitchen—he was not there either—not that she really expected him to be, for all it would soon be lunchtime.

Next she went and knocked at the study door, and waited. When no 'Come in' was to be heard, she began to walk away. Suddenly, though, the door opened.

The instant she saw Nerone, tall, good-looking, and with an expression that was never more serious, all her hard-fought-for control started to disappear. Hastily, as her heart raced and her legs went weak, she grabbed at what control she could, but she could do nothing about the flood of crimson that rushed to her face.

She saw his eyes on her flaming colour and, for one mesmerised moment, she thought she caught a glimpse of something sympathetic and even gentle in his steady, dark-eyed look. She knew herself mistaken, however, when abruptly he spun round and, leaving his study door open, said curtly over his shoulder, 'I take it you've not come to discuss the lunchtime menu!'

His sarcastic comment was just what she needed, though she wasn't about to thank him for it. Stiffened and in control of herself, she followed him inside his study.

'Take a seat,' he offered when, over by the large picture window, he turned to look at her.

'This won't take long,' she told him coolly. 'I've come to tell you I'm leaving.'

'There's no need for that!' Nerone rapped sharply, tossing her an angry look, and suddenly he was all proud, aristocratic Italian as he informed her, 'You need have no fear that I will again forget I'm your host. I will not again touch you . . .'

'I have decided to leave . . .' Jayme tried to get in to repeat forcefully, only to be interrupted again.

'*You* have decided to leave?' he cut in arrogantly, for all the world as though he felt he had a right to make her decisions for her. 'I'm afraid, *signorina*,' he told her toughly, 'that I cannot sanction that.'

'You cannot...?' Jayme gasped, amazed at his nerve. 'I'm perfectly well again now,' she told him, a shade pertly herself, she had to admit, 'and I really can't see anything wrong in you looking after yourself for the remainder of your holiday. So...'

'So *nothing*, *signorina*!' grated Nerone, clearly not liking her arrogance any more than she liked his. 'You are here as my guest, and here you will stay.'

'I'm here as your housekeeper,' she flared, 'but not for much longer!'

'You think I'll allow you to go to this—this Bianco!' Nerone snarled, to her amazement, his chin jutting at an aggressive angle.

'I'm not going to *him*!' she exclaimed in her astonishment, and, starting to grow furious that anyone could think she'd run after any man who had once clearly shown that he didn't want her, she went on angrily, 'For your information, *signore*, I'd only just finished telling him that my purpose in coming to Italy was to tell him, face to face, that I'd changed my mind about wanting to marry him—when you interrupted us!'

'That's why you were holding his hand, was it?' Nerone growled, not looking in any way convinced.

'Oh, I'm leaving!' Jayme spat frustratedly, and turned rapidly around. She was half-way out of the study when suddenly in tones all at once silky, his voice stopped her.

Though it wasn't so much the dramatic change in his manner of speaking that caused her to halt, as the words he spoke. For quite clearly she heard him state,

'I'm sure, *signorina*, that your mother will be most interested to hear the *true version* of all that has happened to you since you arrived in my country.'

Jayme did not merely halt in her flight from the room, but, stunned, her eyes wide, she turned and stared at him open-mouthed.

'You're—not—serious?' she choked from a dry throat.

'But I am,' he replied.

'Y-you don't know her number,' she tried to outface him.

'I dialled it for you once, remember?' he said pleasantly, and, to show he had a numerically retentive brain, he pleasantly repeated it.

'But you wouldn't use it!' Jayme protested in alarm. 'My mother . . .'

'Doesn't know that you've been involved in a motor accident,' Nerone interrupted, adding, 'Because you knew how much it would worry her, you deliberately did not tell her.'

All at once, as she saw the way that this conversation was going, she started to grow desperate. 'I could ring her myself and tell her that I'm fully recovered,' she said agitatedly. 'She . . .'

'Not before I'd rung and acquainted her with how you came off very much the worst when you were hit by a car. Or how, according to Rosa, you were consequently ''black, yellow and blue all over'' as a result of being bounced off the moving vehicle,' he said toughly—and Jayme began to hate him.

The swine! The utter swine! Put like that, it sounded rather dire, and her mother would have forty fits if he told her anything of the kind—and he very well knew that she would do anything to save her mother worry. Lord knew, too, what else he would tell her should her mother mention Tusco's name. Jayme sighed heavily and knew that, hate Nerone Mondadori as she might, she could not allow him to make that call to England. Though she was not yet prepared to give in totally.

'That's blackmail!' she accused hotly.

'Call it what you like,' he shrugged, not a bit daunted. 'But I haven't—made myself responsible for you only to...'.

'You've made yourself responsible for me?' Jayme cut in, astounded.

But it seemed that Nerone had tired of this conversation. 'It was my car that hit you—what else should I do?' he clipped. Then he added, to stagger her more than somewhat, 'Also, what should I do, when I saw you holding hands with your ex-beau and—mistakenly, I now see—believed you had so completely lost your ample supply of pride, other than lend you *my* pride by claiming you—to him—as belonging to me?' Jayme was still surfacing from that when, with a quick glance at his watch, Nerone declared, 'And now it is time for lunch.'

It seemed then as if he was ready for them both to leave his study. Indeed, he had taken a couple of strides from his position by the window before she stopped him.

'Just a minute!'

'Something is wrong, *signorina*?' he queried aloofly.

To her way of thinking, there was a lot wrong, but for the moment she settled for telling him, 'Since it's now obvious to me that my passport has not been handed in to the police, nor will it be, I should like to contact my Consulate with a view to seeing if they can supply me with a new one.'

Nerone favoured her with an arrogant look, then revealed, 'I've already been in touch with your Embassy.'

'You have?' she exclaimed, feeling jolted. 'When?'

'Half an hour ago,' he replied shortly.

'Well?' she queried when he failed to tell her the outcome of his phone call. 'What did they say?'

'It—will take time,' he replied.

'Time? How much time?' she questioned. It was too late now to wish she had contacted the authorities the moment she had realised she did not have her passport.

'First they need some pictures of you,' he replied, and, while she was taking that in, 'We will go to the photographer's this afternoon,' he announced. 'Now, may we eat?' he questioned, just as though he found her extremely tiresome.

Because, even though she was not feeling very well disposed to Nerone, Jayme thought it would be childish on her part to tell him she would eat else-where, they had their meal together. Conversation, however, was very much lacking, for she had nothing she wanted to say to him and he, quite plainly, had nothing he wanted to say to her.

Which was just great as far as she was concerned, Jayme told herself. In fact, it would not bother her if she never exchanged another word with the man again. He was something of a puzzle just the same, though, she mused as she came to the end of her main course. For on the one hand he was insistent that she remain in his home, while on the other it seemed that he had grown so fed up with her that he hadn't waited for her to suggest that she contact her Consulate, but was so anxious to be rid of her that, pipping her at the post, he had already made a call to her Embassy.

He wasn't dragging his feet, either, in that it seemed he wanted her to have those photographs taken at the first opportunity. All of which, she realised, made him a man who did not take his responsibilities lightly.

Which, while everything in her kicked against being regarded as anyone's responsibility, made it difficult for her to understand the feeling of rejection that should suddenly smite her that Nerone could not wait for her to be gone. Which in turn caused her pride to push her up on her high horse when, as she looked over at him, she saw that his glance was on her.

'There isn't any pudding,' she took delight in telling him as she laid down her knife and fork. 'Because of our urgent "appointment in five minutes", the fruit I purchased is still back at that café in Torbole.'

'We can buy more,' he shrugged.

You can go and get it, then! Jayme fumed silently, and, pushing her hand into her pocket, she extracted the money which she had kept separate from her own. 'Your change,' she told him as she placed it on the table, and felt good when the tight-lipped look he gave her showed that she had annoyed him. With a polite, 'Excuse me,' she got up and left the table.

It was around four that afternoon when Nerone came looking for her. By that time, if a trifle subdued, Jayme was no longer in a cross temper. It was a lovely sunny day, and she was in a truly beautiful part of the world. She had spent some time in repeating over and over, 'What can't be cured must be endured,' and in doing so she had decided it would not be long now before she had her new passport. It therefore pleasingly followed that she would not have to endure being blackmailed by this man who seemed determined to believe he had some responsibility for her for much longer either.

Her surmise, however, that she would shortly be in possession of the photographs the Embassy required proved incorrect. For, having sat as instructed while her picture was taken, Jayme had no sooner left her seat than she found that Nerone, with a hand on her elbow, was escorting her out of the photographer's.

'My pictures!' she exclaimed, halting him when it seemed he would have guided her over to his car.

'They won't be ready for a few days,' Nerone told her coolly, and seemed ready to move on.

'A few days?' she exclaimed. 'But . . .'

'I wish it were otherwise, believe me,' he said grimly, going on to explain the fast flow of Italian that had passed between him and the photographer. 'He's working hard to catch up after an extremely busy season and cannot possibly have your pictures ready any sooner.'

It was on the tip of Jayme's tongue to suggest that surely there must be another photographer they could go to. But she had found Nerone's grim, 'I wish it were otherwise, believe me,' deflating enough, without risking his telling her that if one photographer at Lake Garda had had an extremely busy season and was working hard to catch up then that applied, too, to all the other photographers around.

Having found it difficult to understand why she couldn't have her pictures straight away, however, she realised that Nerone must have almost certainly enquired if there was anywhere else they could have an immediate service.

Without further comment she allowed herself to be steered towards the Ferrari. Nor did she have any comment to make when, handing her into the passenger seat, Nerone muttered something about going to get some fruit. He left her to return in a very short while, but Jayme had by then started to grow exceedingly fed up with the situation in general, and was staring out of the side window.

Without a word, Nerone stowed his purchases and got into the car beside her. Without a word, too, he started up the engine and headed the Ferrari back the way they had come.

In silence they made the return journey. But it was at the villa, as Jayme got out of the car and happened to glance Nerone's way, that she saw from his grim expression that when it came to being fed up he seemed to have a head start.

What surprised her, though, was that her subdued mood appeared to have something to do with it. For it seemed to her that Nerone preferred her in a cross temper than in glum humour. At any rate, he soon successfully goaded her back to crossness. Because she could not see any reason at all why he should suddenly decide to bait her.

'Brooding over your lost love, *signorina*?' he suddenly challenged harshly. And when she flicked him a hostile look, but otherwise kept her silence, 'Or perhaps,' he goaded her further, 'he is not so lost.' Then, his expression grimmer than ever, 'Have you arranged to see him again?' he barked.

'No, I haven't!' Jayme answered sharply, unable to keep silent any longer. 'I've told you—it's all over. I've told him...'

What she was saying was drowned under the fury in Nerone's voice when a new thought seemed suddenly to occur to him. 'Have you told him where you're living?' he thundered.

'He's not likely to come calling!' she retorted hotly.

'Have you given him this address?' he insisted aggressively.

'No, I haven't!' Jayme snapped in reply, and as her temper went out of control she spun away from him and headed back down the drive.

'Where the hell are you going?' he bellowed after her.

'Somewhere where I know I'll find peace and quiet!' she yelled back, but did not turn round. Nor did she stop, until she reached 'her place', the public olive grove.

For a while the enchantment she had found before in the olive grove eluded her. To begin with, she was so furious with Nerone Mondadori that all she did was to sit and silently rail against him and his sense of responsibility, that went as far as blackmailing her to ensure that she remain under his roof.

The overbearing swine! she fumed. As if she would give Tusco his address! Hadn't she worked out for herself, before today, that because he was a private sort of man, Nerone would want his address to be kept private?

Jayme was still fuming over Nerone and all his high-handed actions that day, when all at once the smell of wild mint again assailed her nostrils. Then she was lost to everything, for the peace and tranquillity, and the special enchantment of the olive grove, swept over her, and again she was lost. There was then no place in her thoughts for anger and fury.

How long she might have stayed there she didn't know. But suddenly the sound of someone opening the olive grove gate penetrated her thoughts. And then she saw the tall, broad-shouldered shape of Nerone. It was clear that he was looking for her but had not seen her when he took a step in the opposite direction from her. But, although not too long ago she would have grown angry again that his sense of responsibility had caused him to walk down the hill to look for her, that had been before the delight she found in her special place had worked its charm.

She was about to get to her feet and let Nerone know where she was. Then suddenly he about-turned and, as if drawn by a magnet, his glance suddenly went to the far corner of the grove—to the bench where she sat.

Her heart fluttered busily as she watched him move with unhurried but long strides over to her. She had no idea why her heart should behave so peculiarly, but suspected it was because she had spent most of her twenty-two years losing her temper only rarely, while, since she had known Nerone, rarely a day seemed to pass when she wasn't getting heated about something.

Her heart flipped again when Nerone halted by her and looked down into her sea-green eyes. And her feelings towards him were warm as, without a shred of aggressiveness in his voice, he said quietly, 'Come, Jayme, it will be dark soon,' and so saying, extended a hand down to her.

Without conscious thought she lifted her right hand to his left, and stood up. It was not until they had reached the gate that she realised that she still held his hand. Nerone did not make any attempt to hold on to her hand when she eased it away, but she rather thought he too had forgotten they were holding hands like friends.

Together they walked back up the hill, but this time, although no word passed between them, the atmosphere was different. Hostilities between them seemed to have ceased, and Jayme knew she was glad about that.

'I'll just go and have a wash and change, then I'll start on something for dinner,' she told Nerone as, in the hall of the villa, she went to walk away from him.

'I'll come to the kitchen and help,' he said pleasantly.

It amazed Jayme that she could go from liking Nerone to hating him, and back to liking him again, all in the one day. But like him she did when later he helped, as he had promised, to prepare the evening meal. He even seemed to be enjoying himself, she thought, when, smiling, he passed for her inspection a panful of the most misshapen lumps of potato she had ever seen.

'Just right,' she fibbed, and was smiling to herself as she took the pan from him and turned to put it on the stove.

Nerone's eyes were still on her, she observed when she turned back, and for one crazy moment she had the most heart-racing feeling that he wanted to embrace her—perhaps not in a sexual way, but—just wanted to put his arms around her. To show how completely she had got her wires crossed, however, his voice showed he had no such thoughts in his head. 'You just wait until you see the way I set the table!' he said easily. She watched him walk away and knew she had indeed got her wires crossed, but also that had he put his arms around her she would not have protested too much.

Which, she mused when, having disposed of the soup course, they began their second, was most peculiar. She had just cut into a piece of meat and was reflecting that she would do well to check not only the temper which Nerone was so capable of arousing in her, but also any stray whim that might again surface to want to know the security of his arms, when suddenly the phone rang.

'Shall I answer it?' asked Nerone, his look humorous.

'I've a feeling it's not going to stop ringing until you do,' Jayme smiled, and had visions of taking his plate and putting it in the oven to keep warm when, deciding to take the call in the dining-room, he left his place and went over to the phone.

'*Pronto,*' she heard him say, but she understood nothing else. Though, when his call seemed to go on for some time, and she was more seriously thinking in terms of putting his dinner in the oven, she was suddenly turned away from her intention when, in the middle of a spate of Italian, she could have sworn she heard Nerone say her name. She could have been mistaken, of course, and 'Jayme' could have some everyday meaning in Italian, but somehow she didn't think so.

She had done nothing about taking Nerone's dinner to the stove when suddenly his call was over and, his expression thoughtful, he was replacing the receiver. But as he sat down again, his meal was left to lose even more heat because, as he sat down, his glance rested not on his dinner but on his dinner companion. Jayme was convinced from the thoughtful look still in his eyes that she had featured somewhere in his conversation.

In fact, so convinced was she that, when normally nothing would have moved her to be rude enough to enquire who his call was from, it seemed only natural then that she should ask, 'Was that the police?'

'Police?' he questioned in return.

'I'm sorry,' she mumbled quickly, feeling a shade pink, 'I thought I overheard you say my name. I thought it might be something to do with my passport.'

She had lowered her eyes, and was feeling to some degree embarrassed, when Nerone suddenly owned, 'You did hear me speak your name. But I was not speaking with the police,' he went on 'but firstly to my father, and then my mother.'

'You were speaking to your parents, about me?' Jayme gasped, her eyes quickly back on Nerone again.

'Si!' he replied, and to her eyes he looked a little troubled. 'Though to be more precise, it was more that my parents were talking of you than the other way around.'

'But your parents don't know anything about me!' she exclaimed, staring at him incredulously.

'They do now,' he told her, then dropped a bombshell. 'Apparently, so my father tells me, the Press, not knowing where to contact me, have been in touch with him and my mother, to ask for verification of the information they have that I'm engaged to be married.'

'Oh, no!' gasped Jayme. Then, 'Tusco...' she added, and felt honour-bound to reveal, 'Tusco Bianco, he—has friends in journalism. He wanted to work in journalism himself, so he must have contacts...'

She came to a halt when, his tone suddenly sharp, Nerone rapped, 'I've no doubt at all where the story originated!'

'Well, don't blame me!' Jayme said crossly, sensing that all the fault was going to be laid at her door. 'It was you who told Tusco that I was your fiancée, not the other way round!' Angry on the instant, she glared at him. 'Anyhow,' she went on when he looked down his arrogant nose at her for her trouble, 'you've been able to put your parents' minds at rest about your having suddenly acquired a fiancée, so...'

'I,' Nerone cut in icily, 'am not in the habit of lying to my parents!'

'But—we—you—you and I,' Jayme spluttered, 'we're *not* engaged!'

'In order to protect you,' he answered grittily, 'I've told your ex-man friend that we are.'

'Protect me?' Jayme went to protest, but found her comment ignored.

'When my father asked me if I knew an Englishwoman by the name of Jayme Warren, I could not deny it,' Nerone continued. 'When he further asked if I could deny that I had first introduced Signorina Jayme Warren as my betrothed to someone other than my family, I was compelled to tell him that I could not.'

'But,' Jayme got in urgently, 'you explained, you...'

'Before I could do any explaining,' he cut her off, 'my mother, who has been praying for this past ten years that I would take myself a wife so that she may have her heart's desire and have some grandchildren she can spoil—and who was obviously by my father's side listening—was unable to hold back any longer, and had taken the phone from him, ready to forgive me anything. By now,' he stated, 'she will have the two of us married, and will be hoping for nothing less than that in a year from now she will be holding her first grandchild in her arms.'

'Oh, grief!' Jayme groaned.

'I could not,' Nerone responded, 'have phrased it better myself.'

CHAPTER SIX

JAYME spent a restless night, and awoke early on Tuesday with her thoughts straight away on the same treadmill that they had been on during her night-time waking hours.

She had not eaten anything more after Nerone had revealed that his parents now believed them to be engaged. Why his 'I could not have phrased it better myself' should have stung so, she had no notion, but his answer to her 'Oh, grief!' had caused her to re-iterate sharply that it wasn't she who had told Tusco Bianco that they were engaged. She and Nerone had then had a brief argument, during which she had said she couldn't see why he couldn't have explained everything to his mother, and he, all arrogance, had said that his parent had been too excited for him to get another word in. Whereupon, having gone completely off the idea of eating, Jayme had stood up to clear her place, only to find that Nerone had lost his appetite too. Together they had cleared the dining-room table and together they had loaded up the dishwasher. Then, with a taut goodnight, she had left him and gone to bed—if Nerone had replied to her goodnight, she hadn't heard it.

Swine! she dubbed him as she got out of bed and went to run her bath. He could jolly well ring his parents today and explain everything, she fumed as she tested the temperature of the water. Though how she was going to get him to do that, when she had quickly learned that he was a man who was a law unto himself, she was not sure.

Jayme dawdled over her bath, and made no attempt to speed up as she donned a cotton dress and sandals and ran a comb through her platinum-blonde hair. She might be his acting housekeeper, his—for the moment—mock fiancée, and blackmailed to stay convalescent beneath his roof into the bargain, but today she was in no hurry to get on with her chores, light though those chores were. There was bound to be friction between her and Nerone the moment she opened her mouth to 'suggest' that it might be an idea if he rang his parents—and, oddly, she had just discovered that there was some peculiar part of her that just did not want to war with him!

It was then that Jayme put a spurt on. Hurriedly she left her room. Grief, she wasn't afraid of doing battle with him! Why... She opened the kitchen door, and her thoughts ceased. Nerone was there, and he was making a start on getting the breakfast together, and just when she was getting ready to begin hostilities he took the wind right out of her sails. For, when he had not been able to spare her a word in parting last night, this morning he eyed the picture she made—tall, slender, with excellent bone-structure and unusual hair colouring that owed nothing to the hairdresser—and gently he smiled.

Then—and with a good deal of charm—he said softly, 'Good morning, Jayme,' and added, 'How beautiful you are.'

'Why—er—thank you,' she found herself replying, and even though she grew aware that she was in danger of being swamped by his charm, '*Buon giorno*, Nerone,' she greeted him pleasantly.

'Today I thought we'd...' he began, but just then they both heard the sound of a car coming up the drive, and he broke off.

Looking at him, Jayme saw the alert look that entered his intelligent eyes. She guessed then that in all probability he had recognised the sound of the car engine and had a good idea of who was calling— before breakfast. But as the look on his face grew thoughtful, and just when she had begun to wonder if maybe it was someone bringing Rosa back, Nerone appeared to have come to some sort of decision. Then, as the doorbell pealed, his eyes returned to her.

'If I'm not very much mistaken, Jayme,' he said quietly, 'my parents have decided to pay us a visit.'

'Your parents?' she repeated in some agitation.

'Do not be alarmed,' he murmured as he went towards the hall door. 'I promise you, they will not eat you.'

It was all very well for him to tell her not to be alarmed, she thought as she heard the front door was open and a mature female voice break into a stream of excited Italian. But right now, unless Nerone was telling his mother, on the doorstep, that he was not engaged to be married, Jayme had no idea how she should act.

Realising that since Signora Mondadori seemed to set great store on Nerone's at last letting himself get caught, and that he might want to break it to her gently that she had got so excited for nothing, Jayme was still pondering how she should act when a pleased new male voice made some comment, and the voice seemed much nearer.

'Jayme,' said Nerone as he led the way into the kitchen with every appearance of being extremely happy, 'my mother and father have come especially from Turin to meet you.'

Jayme no longer had to think how to act—instinct took over. The mere fact that Nerone's parents were obviously so keen to meet their future daughter-in-law that they must have left their Turin home before dawn broke had a lot to do with it. But what caused Jayme, for the moment, to be swept along with a dishonesty which she felt was none of her making was the look of sheer joy on the face of the tall and elegant woman of about sixty who stepped out from just behind Nerone.

'Jayme,' she murmured her name, and there were tears welling in her eyes as, clearly tremendously moved, the expensively clad woman took hold of her two hands and breathed some heartfelt words in Italian.

'Jayme doesn't speak Italian, *Madre*,' Nerone cut in and, in fine good humour, he turned to Jayme and translated. 'My mother, as I myself told you only a few minutes ago, *cara*, says that you are very beautiful,' and while Jayme was doing her best not to look startled by the fact that quite plainly he was not going to disabuse his parents of the idea that they were engaged, Nerone went on to make the introductions formally.

Then first Jayme was embraced by Concetta Mondadori, who kissed her on both cheeks and cried, in excellent English, 'Oh, Jayme, you cannot know how full of joy my heart is to meet you!'

'I—er...' Jayme tried, but anything she might or might not have said was buried by Nerone formally introducing his father.

Enéa Mondadori was a man of some charm, and was almost as tall as his son. Like his wife, he kissed

Jayme on both cheeks, then stood back, to say handsomely, 'As both my wife and my son have already observed, you are very beautiful.' He paused, then smiled and said, 'Welcome into my family, Jayme.'

Jayme felt deeply moved by what he had just said, but, because she knew that soon either she or Nerone would have to tell these lovely people that she was never likely to become a member of the Mondadori family, she looked, a little helplessly, towards Nerone. He did not fail her. Though nor did he say anything like what she thought he should.

Instead, he told his parents, 'Jayme and I were just about to have breakfast. We've been in the habit of eating in the kitchen, but,' he smiled teasingly at his mother, 'now you are here, I suspect we had better set the breakfast-room table for four.'

'It was your mother's opinion that we should arrive in time for breakfast,' his father murmured drily, but as he and his son exchanged amused glances, suddenly Concetta Mondadori, sounding far from amused, was saying,

'Jayme is living here with you, Nerone?'

All sign of amusement rapidly left him. 'She is,' he said firmly, and went on, his expression extremely serious, 'It was my wish that Jayme stay here with me.'

And while Jayme realised that clearly Signora Mondadori was not happy about this state of affairs, and also that Nerone did not appear to like his mother's attitude, the elegant Italian lady was pressing on, 'But Rosa is here to chaperon you?'

'Rosa is on holiday,' Nerone replied, surprising Jayme that he should call Rosa's going to look after her daughter a holiday. Though Jayme forgot all about the housekeeper when, most firmly, Nerone told his mother, 'But you have no need to worry. A chaperon is not required!'

'I have your word on that, my son?' his mother, a most forthright woman, Jayme was learning, queried.

'*Si!*' he told her, and added something else in Italian which, whether he expected it or not, made his mother suddenly all smiles again. She turned to Jayme, apologised and translated.

'Forgive me, dear Jayme,' she smiled, 'but in the absence of your mother being here, I feel I have some duty to her. But,' she went on, 'Nerone has just now told me that although it was reluctantly that you have agreed to stay here, your very innocence is your chaperon.'

'Er...' Jayme swallowed, 'really,' she murmured, doing her best to get used to the openness of this Italian family, while at the same time realising that to tell his mother what he had must mean that Nerone was still bent on protecting her—just as yesterday when, to protect her, he had told Tusco they were engaged.

Because of her lack of knowledge of the Italian language, everyone, with only the occasional lapse, spoke English over breakfast. On the one hand Jayme felt more relaxed at being able to comprehend what was being said. But, on the other, she was growing rather anxious expecting that at any moment—as he surely would—Nerone would get round to telling his parents that they weren't actually engaged—or actually, anything.

As the minutes ticked by, however, she started to grow more and more of the opinion that Nerone had no intention of telling his parents anything of the sort. That impression became certainty when, there having been a number of occasions when he could have said something, they were finishing off their coffee and still not a word had been said.

'Is this your first visit to Italy, Jayme?' Concetta Mondadori enquired with a warm smile.

'Yes, I . . .' Jayme began, but before she could add more, Nerone, who she later realised was taking steps to head off what almost certainly would be his mother's next question as to where had they met, was butting in.

'Talking of visits, *Madre*, you should have let me know you were coming.'

'You would rather we had not come?' his mother questioned in her forthright way.

'You know I'm delighted to see you,' Nerone immediately teased his parent. 'Had I been expecting you, however, I would never have planned to show Jayme something of our country today.'

It was news to Jayme that he had planned to show her anything of Italy that day. But as Signora Mondadori broke into hurried Italian—before she recollected that Jayme could not understand her—Jayme remembered that Nerone had been saying something about, 'Today, I thought we'd . . .' when he had heard his parents arriving.

'I apologise,' his mother switched to English, then insisted, 'Your father and I should not like at all for you to change your plans because of us. Since this is Jayme's first time in Italy, there is much she will want to see.'

'That's—true,' Jayme had to admit as three pairs of eyes looked in her direction, plainly expecting her to make some reply. She looked at Nerone and he smiled, encouragingly. She looked away.

'So you must do whatever you have plans to do, just as if Enéa and I were not here,' Signora

Mondadori went on. 'You go when you are ready, and I will have a good Italian meal waiting for you when you return.'

'You will stay for a while?' Nerone teased her, and obviously very much in harmony with his father, for his mouth twitched when his father smirked and murmured,

'Your mother had her suitcase packed, and mine, within an hour of our speaking with you last night.'

Concetta Mondadori gave both men a speaking look. 'You see what I have to put up with!' she sighed, then suddenly laughed, and all at once Jayme knew that she liked this woman. Which, only a minute later, made it dreadfully difficult not to burst out with the truth of her non-engagement to Nerone, when his mother, her own hands adorned by two most exquisite diamond rings, one a large but tasteful solitaire, the other a half-hoop of seven stones, suddenly noticed that Jayme's hands were ringless. 'Where is your engagement ring?' she asked in some surprise.

'Our engagement is not official yet, *Madre*,' Nerone told his mother easily, and while Jayme could only stare at this man who only last night had told her icily, 'I'm not in the habit of lying to my parents,' he went on. 'The Press got hold of our news before Jayme and I had even discussed what sort of ring she would like.'

Jayme stared at Nerone in some amazement, but as a brief free-for-all broke out among the Mondadoris as they discussed some members of the Press she had time to hide her amazement. Then Nerone was pushing his chair back from the table.

'The day will be gone if Jayme and I don't soon get started,' he commented, and would have begun carrying some of the breakfast things back to the kitchen had his mother not stopped him.

'You go,' she said happily. 'Your father and I will attend to the dishes.'

'You see the sacrifices I make for you, my son?' his father intoned drolly, and while Jayme could not help but smile and—yes, even realise that she could enjoy being a part of this family—Nerone's mother was enquiring which part of Italy Nerone had it in mind to show his fiancée that day.

'Venice,' he replied as he went round to Jayme's chair to pull it back for her.

'Venice?' Concetta Mondadori exclaimed. 'In the rain?'

'Venice is beautiful at any time,' Nerone replied, and only then, with so much else having happened that morning, did Jayme realise that there had been a change in the weather, and that the rain was fairly pouring down.

The rain was the last thing on her mind, though, when some fifteen minutes later she was sitting beside Nerone in his Ferrari as he steered it down the drive from his villa. She had to own that to be able to see Venice, which she thought must be some hours' drive away, had very considerable appeal. But what had more appeal, as Nerone drove out on to the main road and left his villa behind, was the need to find out from him just what he thought he was playing at.

She half turned in her seat to look at him, then opened her mouth, only to find that he had got in first. 'It was good of you to wait this long,' he remarked pleasantly, succeeding to some extent, whether he knew it or not, in disarming her.

'What . . .?' she began to question.

'I have experienced a little of your temper, Jayme,' he said charmingly, and disarmed her a little more, 'which is why I thank you most sincerely for not— er—tearing into me in front of my family.'

'You had no right to—to let your parents continue to believe that you and I are engaged,' was the best she could come up with in the way of censure. And, as it came to her that she was not being strict enough, 'No right at all!' she told him severely.

'You are right, of course,' he defeated her by agreeing with her. 'But then you did not see, as I did, my mother's joyous expression when I opened the door to her.'

'Even so...' Jayme began to protest, but found she must have spoken in too quiet a voice, for Nerone could not have heard her, since he went on,

'Forgive me for wanting to see her happy, Jayme. Last year, when she was in hospital...' he said, and his tone was so grave that Jayme instantly knew he had feared for his mother's life.

'Your mother was seriously ill?' she questioned.

'After her surgery, my father and I...'

'Oh, Nerone!' Jayme breathed softly. Clearly his mother must have been quite desperately ill last year and must have needed major surgery, she realised. She had seen for herself, in the fond way both Nerone and his father teased Signora Mondadori, that they loved her very much. They must have gone through a quite dreadful time while she had been fighting to live. It was hardly surprising, she acknowledged, that on seeing his mother so overjoyed that morning he had not been able to tell her the truth. It was wrong, of course, and there was no saying differently. But, Jayme thought, thinking of how all of this had got started, Nerone hadn't known that Tusco Bianco had

journalist friends when—to protect her when believing she would bitterly regret having anything more
to do with Tusco once her pride had returned—he had
claimed her as his fiancée. 'Your mother will have to
know the truth some time,' she told Nerone, realising
that he had not pressured her, but had left her to work
it out for herself.

'I know,' he answered quietly, 'but not for a little
while. For a little while let her...'

'But I'm not sure that I'm very good at deceiving
people,' Jayme interrupted.

'You deceived your friend Bianco into believing
you'd come to Italy to tell him to his face that you
couldn't marry him,' Nerone commented coolly.

'Well, he would believe it, wouldn't he!' snapped
Jayme, sensing criticism in Nerone's cool remark.
'Despite his little show of dramatics, he believed me
because, in truth, he wanted to believe me. He'd...'

'As my mother will believe because she wants to
believe, and wishes to have you some day for her
daughter. But,' he went on swiftly, turning to look at
Jayme for a moment and catching the antagonistic
look she threw him, 'for your sake, and because I
know that in your heart to act a lie is difficult for
you, I have brought you away from the villa for the
day.'

'Oh,' murmured Jayme, and was not very sure how
she felt about the 'for your sake.' Quite plainly Nerone
Mondadori was not driving her to Venice from any
particular wish to do so. Though, because she was too
proud to show him that she felt a little miffed, she
enquired, 'Might I ask why?' as though she had not
much interest in his answer.

'It seemed the best thing to do,' he replied. 'If I
know my parents, they will stay for a week or so. If

I take you out somewhere every day, you will be away from the villa, where any natural questions my mother might ask could make you feel uncomfortable.'

'I hope,' Jayme told him coolly, 'that I'll be back in England long before the "week or so" your parents will be with you is over.'

'I'm doing my best in that direction, Jayme,' he told her quietly, and, had she not known better, she realised that the sensation that came over her that all too obviously Nerone could not wait for her to be gone—his self-appointed responsibility for her over— might have been one of pique.

She gave him a speaking look. 'Perhaps I'd better send some postcards from Venice,' she mumbled.

'You do not wish to telephone your mother?'

Jayme shook her head. 'I've phoned her twice, and as you remarked once, Nerone, I've already lied to my mother by omission—I don't want to run the risk of maybe having to lie by word.'

'Then we will make our first errand in Venice to send some postcards,' he said, and Jayme could not be sure, but she felt that his tones held more warmth than previously.

Perhaps that imagined warmth was responsible for a thaw setting in in her too. Because, although from the way things had been going a short while ago she would not have been surprised had they arrived in Venice as arch-enemies, she discovered when they did arrive and park the car that, just as Nerone's manner to her was friendly, her manner to him was friendly in return.

'Picture postcards, I think we said,' he smiled down at her. Then, as she stared up at him, he murmured, 'You are remarkable, Jayme—even with the rain pouring down on you, you manage to look most stunning.'

'It's a gift,' she said, and grinned, and quite thought then—ridiculously, she realised later—that Nerone was going to bend his head and kiss her. Ridiculously too, as his glance went from her eyes to her lips, her heart fluttered. Then, in the next moment, Nerone had spun about and was exchanging lire for a couple of plastic macs with which some enterprising tradesman was doing a roaring business. 'Do I still look stunning?' she could not resist asking Nerone when she had the shapeless garment about her.

'You'd look good in a sugar sack, and you know it,' he replied. Then, 'Postcards,' he said decisively, 'then lunch.'

Quite when Jayme began to feel happy, she didn't know. It probably began when the wonder that was Venice started to seep through her bones. At first, though, as Nerone took her to buy the cards she wanted, Venice seemed to her to be a mass of small alleyways and shops. Then suddenly the very atmosphere of the place started to get to her.

Nerone, to her surprise, turned out to be the soul of patience and waited with not the smallest sign that he was not enjoying doing what he was doing. 'That's about it,' Jayme told him, and at his request she handed her three cards to him and watched in amused surprise as he read the message on the top card—the one to Michelle—which read 'In Venice for the day—Venice is super!' 'Do you always read other people's mail?' she queried when he came back from posting the cards.

'Always,' he smiled, unabashed, and Jayme could not help it, she burst out laughing.

The smart restaurant which Nerone took her to was crowded. Yet somehow he got them a table for two, and they were soon both studying the menu. 'I'll start with the spaghetti, I think,' Jayme, determined to eat 'Italian' today, told Nerone when he asked if she had a preference. 'Then after that I'll have the—er—um—*bollito misto.*' she got her tongue round the Italian menu.

'That's the manager,' Nerone told her, his expression deadpan.

Jayme looked at him, and liked him, and liked the mischief lurking in his eyes. 'Well,' she replied, 'if Signor Bollito Misto doesn't mind . . .' and liked him more and more when this time he burst out laughing.

Bollito misto, when it arrived, turned out to be a selection of mixed boiled meats—and was enormous. Having ordered such a plateful, however, Jayme could see that there was only one way in which she could save her face. She ploughed her way through it, and earned herself a warm 'Bravo!' from Nerone for her efforts.

'Could we walk—like, say, for about eight hours?' she asked as they left the restaurant, feeling sorely in need of some exercise.

'For you, anything,' he replied lightly as he turned to her and pulled the edges of her waterproof closer around her.

Jayme smiled, and for the next hour or so she went wherever he led. Her impressions then were many and varied. They crossed the Grand Canal by way of the Rialto Bridge, which had three spans and two rows of shops. Jayme unhurriedly dallied and window-shopped, and to her pleasure it seemed as though Nerone had really meant it when he had said, 'For you, anything,' because he did not appear to mind one tiny bit—indeed, he seemed to be looking and seeing and savouring and generally enjoying the experience as much as she.

'Where are the gondolas?' she asked as they walked on. By then she had seen several sections of waterways—but not one gondola.

'I fear the boats will not run in this weather,' Nerone replied.

'Of course,' Jayme smiled, realising that she should have worked that out for herself.

'You wanted to ride in a gondola?'

'Doesn't everyone?' she laughed.

'We will return,' Nerone promised, 'and you shall have your gondola ride.'

They carried on walking, and Jayme thought he must mean that, if the weather cleared up that afternoon, they would return to a gondola harbour, and hire one of the craft.

The weather did not clear up, though. But as they reached St Mark's Square she was struck by the fact that the incessant rain did not deter the hundreds of pigeons there from plodding from one visitor to the square to another in search of pickings.

By that time, though, Jayme was totally captivated by Venice. She stood with Nerone and, despite the rain, gazed enrapt. Only when her companion murmured quietly in her ear, 'Come, *cara*, you are getting drenched,' did she realise that it had started to rain more heavily than before.

She had discovered that her heart was racing when, escorting her out of the rain, Nerone, with his hand on her arm, piloted her to one of the historical buildings. For a moment it crazily occurred to her that his quietly spoken endearment was responsible for the increase in her heart-rate. Then, having decided that she was being ridiculous and that Nerone had not called her 'dear' from any feeling of affection, but more probably because her name had escaped him for an instant, Jayme wondered if that tingly feeling she had experienced when his hand had firmly taken her arm had anything to do with her heart deciding to increase its pace. She scrapped both ideas in favour of—whose heart wouldn't hurry up a few beats? She was in Venice, for goodness' sake!

'Where's this?' she asked Nerone when he had paid an entrance fee and was escorting her up a wide staircase.

'The Doge's Palace,' he replied, and escorted her from room to room, pausing when she did to admire a painting, and, again in no hurry, keeping slow pace with her.

Nerone, Jayme discovered, was a fund of information, and was able to answer each and every one of the questions that popped into her head. As with a lot of history, though, some of the answers to her questions were not as rosy as she had imagined.

They had reached the Bridge of Sighs when, fondly imagining that the enclosed bridge led to the apartments of ladies who sighed as they waited for the men they loved to call, she was disabused of that idea.

'The bridge was built to connect the palace with the dungeons,' he enlightened her, in answer to her question.

'Oh!' Jayme murmured, disappointed. 'And—the sighs?'

'Were those of the prisoners as they crossed it while waiting to be sentenced, I'm afraid,' Nerone told her as he scrutinised her, for the moment, solemn face.

'Did no one ever escape?' she enquired as she moved to the small apertures in some concrete artwork of the bridge that were part of tiny windows.

She was peering down below, where a canal flowed and where by raising her eyes she could make out three small bridges, when Nerone answered, 'It's said that Casanova made it to freedom dressed in some female attire brought to him by one of his visitors.'

When they left the Ducal Palace the light on that most inclement day had started to fade, and Jayme knew they must shortly make their way back to Lake Garda.

'I've enjoyed myself tremendously,' she told Nerone, and saw him smile as if it pleased him, when clearly it seemed that she had never expected to enjoy her day out with him, that she should confess that she had.

'I believe we've time for a cup of your English tea before we leave,' he told her pleasantly, and Jayme had more enjoyment when, with a canopy of tarpaulin preventing the rain from soaking them, they sat outside a café and drank tea while a nearby band of musicians played quietly in the background. Jayme felt her day was a squirrel's store of happy memories.

Nor were her happy memories over. For when she and Nerone arrived back at the villa, his parents were there to greet them, and Jayme thought them lovely people. And she had to own that she enjoyed being mothered by Concetta Mondadori when, having heard from her son how it had rained non-stop in Venice, she at once enquired, 'You got wet, Jayme?'

'A little,' Jayme owned, and felt warmed when the *signora*, who had been so ill herself, said something sharp to her son on the subject of his fiancée catching a chill, then suggested that she had time to have a hot bath before dinner. Jayme went to do as she suggested, but not before she had seen the traces of amusement lurking around Nerone's mouth. It pleased her that he seemed happy.

Dinner that night was a cheerful affair. Jayme had thought that after her mammoth lunch she would not want to eat again for a week. But that was before she had tasted the turkey Tetrazzini which Nerone's mother had prepared. As well as turkey in the delicious recipe, there were mushrooms and spaghetti which, mixed with sherry and cream, plus a dash of other ingredients, gave turkey a new meaning.

'I couldn't eat another crumb!' Jayme exclaimed when Concetta Mondadori wanted her to have seconds.

'But there's nothing of you!' the *signora* complained.

'Perhaps Jayme likes it that way,' Nerone intervened. 'But, since I have a bigger frame to fill,' he addressed his mother, 'may I have my fiancée's share?'

A little startled to hear him so easily call her his fiancée, Jayme stared at him. Her attention was diverted though, when his mother asked her if her mother did any cooking.

'Oh, yes,' she replied, and, refraining from saying that in her mother's case cooking was not a hobby— as she suspected was the case with Nerone's mother— but a necessity, she smiled, 'She too is a good cook.'

'As is her daughter,' Nerone put in.

'You never said,' Jayme felt lighthearted enough to tease, and loved it when he suddenly grinned. 'Er— my mother taught all three of us to cook,' she went on, dragging her attention abruptly from him.

'There are three of you?' Signora Mondadori enquired, and was so obviously interested that Jayme could see no reason to hold back from answering.

'I have two sisters, Michelle and Leonie,' she replied. 'Leonie's fourteen and attends the local school, and Michelle, who has a fine brain, hopes to go to university.'

'And you, Jayme,' Nerone's mother asked, 'how do you fill your day? Do you perhaps have a job?'

'Oh, yes,' Jayme replied cheerfully. 'I work as a secretary. I...'

'Jayme has worked since she was sixteen,' Nerone cut in, and to her astonishment he added quietly, 'And I'm very proud of her.'

Pink colour had crept beneath her skin before it dawned on her that Nerone's remark must have stemmed from some belief that as a 'fiancé', he ought to say something nice about or to her every now and then. But, since all eyes were now on her—and her blush—and since Nerone's mother was looking at her warm skin colour as though delighted that anyone still blushed these days, Jayme found herself rushing into speech and saying the first thing that came into her head.

'My father died when I was sixteen, so it was—er—necessary for us all to make changes. My mother most of all, though.'

'Are you saying that your finances suffered on the death of your father?' Enéa Mondadori enquired shrewdly.

'My father never expected to die so young,' Jayme replied. 'Anyhow,' she went on swiftly, 'my mother coped marvellously, and turned our home, which fortunately is a large one,' she inserted with a touch of humour, 'into a guesthouse.'

'Ah,' Concetta Mondadori murmured, 'I think your mother must be a lady of great courage,' and Jayme no longer wondered why, when anything connected with her family had always been private before, she should now have revealed as much as she had. For, even without the genuine warmth she had heard in the *signora*'s voice, Jayme realised that she felt among friends.

Shortly after thanking the woman she now regarded as her hostess for her splendid meal, Jayme decided to go to bed. For the most part it had been a really splendid day, but she was suddenly starting to feel the most upsetting, peculiar sensation of something disturbing—yet something she could not exactly put her finger on.

Having just said goodnight to Nerone's mother and father, however, when Jayme flicked a glance at Nerone, it was to see that he too was on his feet and was walking over to where she stood.

'*Buona notte*, Nerone,' she bade him pleasantly as she realised that because of his parents being there he might, in true Italian fashion, kiss her on both cheeks as he returned her *buona notte*.

'Goodnight, *cara*,' he said softly, and then, after a moment or two of looking deeply into her eyes, his head started to come down and gently he kissed her on the mouth.

Jayme went quickly to her room. Quietly she closed the door. Then a breathless sigh left her. She'd had a marvellous day. A happy day. She had met Nerone's mother and father, and she had liked them. But what was more shaking than disturbing was the fact that she had just realised what that something was which she had found most upsetting,. but hadn't been able to put her finger on.

For, to rock her to her foundations, she had just realised, from the moment that Nerone's warm and tender mouth had gently lain over hers just now, that while she liked Enéa and Concetta Mondadori—she was in love with their son!

CHAPTER SEVEN

THE sunny weather was back the next day. Jayme awoke to find the sun streaming in through her bedroom window. She had awakened later than usual, and that did not surprise her. She had spent a fitful night, with the new discovery that she loved Nerone bringing her to the surface of wakefulness many times.

She bathed and dressed with the all-consuming emotion she felt for Nerone Mondadori still with her. She knew it would not go away. She had thought she had been in love before—she now knew she had not. Being in love with Tusco Bianco had never felt like this. What she had felt for Tusco was feeble by comparison.

Dully, she realised that Nerone would never love her, but she took heart from the thought that he seemed to like her. At least, given that he had been more or less obliged to take her out yesterday, she hadn't had the feeling that he felt it too much of a chore. Her spirits took a downward dip again as the thought came to her that a man of Nerone's sophistication was hardly likely to let her see him yawning with boredom throughout the whole day, was he?

Swiftly she seated herself in front of her dressing-table mirror and brushed her long platinum-blonde hair. She was clad in crisp white trousers and an eau-de-Nil-coloured T-shirt. She felt a great urgency within her to see Nerone again, but at the same time she felt too constrained, by an unexpected shyness, to move.

Love, true love, was murder on the emotions, she was fast realising when, her palms feeling moist, she made herself leave her room. She went towards the kitchen knowing the uselessness of wishing it were yesterday again. Yesterday when although, as she now realised, there were definite signs that something momentous was happening with regard to her affections, she had not yet recognised the extent of her caring for Nerone.

She went into the kitchen aware that no matter how much she might prefer not to be in love with Nerone, there was not the smallest thing she could do about it. Her feelings for him were out of her control.

'Jayme!' Concetta Mondadori looked up from slicing bread to greet her warmly. 'You slept well, hmm?'

'I'm sorry I'm late,' Jayme apologised instantly, but soon realised, when Signora Mondadori would not let her do a thing to help, that her hostess's enquiry had been a genuine one.

'I can manage quite well here,' the Italian woman beamed at her. 'Why not go to the breakfast-room?' she suggested. 'There is a certain man there who I am sure is impatient to see you.'

Jayme smiled back, because she couldn't see what else she could do. Then, pausing to lift up a tray containing plates of bread and meats, she went to the breakfast-room, wishing Nerone could be half as impatient to see her as she was to see him.

Both father and son were in the room when she entered, and Enéa Mondadori's greeting to her was as warm as his wife's. 'Good morning, Jayme,' he bade her, and with natural charm, 'You have brought the sun out today, I see.'

'Good morning,' she replied and, liking this family, she smiled.

'Good morning,' Nerone had come over to her, but suddenly Jayme was all nerves in case he intended to start the day in the same way in which he had ended yesterday.

'Good morning, Nerone,' she murmured, and, not sure how she would react at feeling his warm mouth gentle over hers again, she avoided looking into his eyes, realised that she still had the tray in her hands, and pushed it towards him.

Automatically, it seemed, he took it from her, but he did not at once move away, she noticed. She was aware by then that he was standing looking at her and, simply because she could not help it, she had to look at him.

His expression was serious, she observed, as silently he stared into the sea-green depths of her eyes. Jayme's heart pumped painfully as, afraid of giving away how very much in love with him she was, she looked away from him. Fortunately though, just at that moment Signora Mondadori arrived with the remainder of the breakfast. 'I forgot the coffee-pot,' she commented, and as Nerone transferred the contents of the tray to the table and then went to collect the coffee, Jayme slid into her usual seat.

She was in dread at the start of that meal that she might slip up in an unthinking way, and might reveal some of what was in her heart. But as breakfast progressed, and Signora Mondadori showed that she was as full of conversation as she had been at breakfast yesterday, Jayme's fears started to fade.

When none of the *signora*'s topics of discussion centred on her son or the woman she believed he was to marry, Jayme grew more relaxed still. Which left

her vulnerable and totally without an answer when
the older woman turned to her and enquired, 'And
where are you and Nerone going today, Jayme?'

'I...' Jayme replied blankly, 'I—er—don't think
we're going any...'

'I thought I'd show Jayme a little of Verona today,'
Nerone cut in smoothly. 'Would you like that, my
dear?' he enquired—and seemed to be daring her to
say no.

Yesterday Jayme thought she might have bridled at
him challenging her in such a way. But that was yesterday. On their outing then she had not recognised
where her heart lay. Today she knew exactly where it
lodged and who, without knowing it, held it. And
although only minutes ago she had been terrified that
by some unthought word, look or deed she might slip
up and reveal her love, suddenly she was swamped by
a yearning to have another day out with him.

'I'd like to see Verona very much, please,' she told
him, looking not at him but at her coffee-cup. Picking
up her cup, she took a sip.

When a short while later she returned to her room
prior to going out to the Ferrari, Jayme had started
to get excited at the prospect of another whole day
spent with Nerone. Just one day, sang her heart.
Surely, since soon she would return to England, never
to see him again, she could have just one day?

They did not go to Verona straight away. For while
she was doing her best to act naturally, and as she
would have acted yesterday, no sooner had they left
the villa than, part from curiosity, part because she
wanted to imagine Nerone here in Lake Garda, she
started to ask questions about this region where he
had his holiday home.

'Is Lake Garda very big?' she asked, as he steered his car down towards the main road.

'It's the largest lake in Italy,' he replied, and seemed suddenly in the same good humour he had been in yesterday as he added, 'Would you like for us to drive around it?'

'Have we time?' she enquired.

'It will probably take the rest of the morning to do the ninety or so miles, but,' he turned and gave her a friendly look that tilted her heart, 'we can see Verona this afternoon.'

'Can we?' she asked, and the matter was settled.

The morning flew by. Lake Garda was a paradise of scenery, of high green mountains, of soaring vistas of craggy limestone rock and of lush vegetation. Cypress trees abounded, and Jayme stored up memory after memory. They passed through any number of thriving communities where it seemed that each and every house had balconies full of trailing pink and red geraniums. Jayme garnered place names such as Malcesine, Limone and the peninsula of Sirmione, and could only wonder at the engineering achievement of the many roads tunnelled in the mountainous rock through which they sometimes travelled.

When they stopped for lunch, she had at the forefront of her mind the mammoth meals she had eaten yesterday. She had an idea that Signora Mondadori thought her thin and might have another large, though simply delicious, meal waiting that evening.

'Can I just have a small portion of lasagne?' she asked, when Nerone enquired what she had chosen from the menu.

For some seconds he looked silently at her. Then, just as if he had read her mind and knew her feeling that four giant meals in two days would finish her, his mouth started to tug upwards at the corners.

'I shall have the same,' he announced, and grinned, and if it was possible, at that moment Jayme fell even more in love with him.

The journey to Verona took about an hour. Jayme had visited Verona briefly in her search for Tusco Bianco, but this time it was as though she had never before been there. She had certainly never visited the places which Nerone took her to, at any rate.

As Rome had seven hills, little Rome, as Verona was known, he told her, had two hills—St Peter's Hill and Leonardo's Hill. It was up Leonardo's Hill that they drove first to take a look at Verona from above. Jayme was enraptured when, having parked the car, Nerone guided her to a parapet where spread before them was a vista of pinky-brown-roofed, white-fronted houses, tall spires and towers, trees and greenery and, winding its way through the city, the river Adige.

'Now what would you like to see?' he enquired as she looked and looked, and looked some more at the splendid panorama. But it seemed that he did not seriously require an answer, for soon they were driving down the hill.

Once they were on level ground, he again parked the car, and Jayme was brimful with happiness and pride when, taking hold of her arm, the tall and aristocratic-looking Italian kept her close by him as he escorted her through streets that were sometimes cobbled and sometimes not.

They were in Cappello Street when, as Jayme had begun to wonder where he was taking her, they turned into a courtyard and halted. 'Do you know your Romeo and Juliet?' asked Nerone, and pointed to the first-floor stone balcony on the outside of the brick-built house.

'Ohh!' Jayme sighed, and didn't mind just then that Nerone must suspect that she had a soft, romantic heart to have brought her to see Juliet's balcony. 'I know Shakespeare's version,' she turned to answer his question—and discovered that he had not been looking at the balcony but at her.

'The true version of Juliet Capelletti and Romeo Montecchi may be a little different, I fear,' he told her as he smiled down into her eyes.

Jayme's heart somersaulted, and she swiftly decided that she would be better employed in staring at the balcony than into Nerone's eyes. Again he let her take in the balcony and its courtyard, and the profusion of ivy that grew on one wall, for as long as she cared. Then she was feeling the same thrill of Nerone capturing her arm and of pride as together they left the Via Cappello.

The afternoon was going on and the best of the light was gone when, as they strolled through an arcade of expensive-looking shops, Nerone suggested some refreshment. 'I'd like that,' she told him, but was so in love with him, she knew she would have agreed had he suggested anything as outlandish as that they take a dip in the river Adige.

The enchantment of that day continued for Jayme when, in an outside café in the Piazzo Bra, she sat with Nerone and sipped tea while but a stone's throw away stood the magnificent and vast Roman amphitheatre.

All in all, it had been a perfectly wonderful day, she reflected when, back in the car, Nerone headed the Ferrari in the direction of Lake Garda. Not one cross word had they exchanged, and—she hoped it wasn't just her imagination—but it seemed to her that Nerone had enjoyed this day too.

The Ferrari made short work of the return trip, and outside the villa Jayme looked at Nerone. 'Thank you for Lake Garda, and thank you for Verona,' she told him with quiet sincerity.

'Thank you,' he responded, and with quiet charm, he added, 'for—Jayme.'

She walked into the villa with her heart bursting. He did like her, she was sure of it! Hadn't his 'Thank you, for—Jayme' just now meant that?

'Ah—Jayme!' Concetta Mondadori came from the kitchen to greet her. 'You have had a happy day, yes?'

'Oh, yes,' Jayme sighed, and, realising that her reply had sounded too heartfelt, she was glad that Nerone had delayed entering the villa to garage the Ferrari. 'I'll just go and change,' she told Nerone's beaming mother as a delicious smell of something cooking wafted from the kitchen.

In her room, Jayme had a quick shower, and changed from the trousers and T-shirt she had worn all day into a straight-skirted dress of blue linen.

Having had the one more day she had wanted with Nerone—a day that, for her, had turned out to be quite blissful—Jayme joined the kind Mondadori family for dinner with a heart full of hope that the evening would continue in the same blissful way.

It seemed that her hope would be fulfilled when over the first course conversation was cheerful, and mostly about Lake Garda. The happy atmosphere continued while they ate a second course of *oca con mele e castagne*, the most mouthwatering goose with apple and chestnuts which Jayme had ever tasted.

Over the final course of stuffed peaches, Jayme savoured every moment of sharing with Nerone and his family what she felt to be exquisite harmony. An exquisite harmony which, she felt too, it would be criminal to break.

Which, when at that moment she was convinced that she would go to great lengths not to spoil the atmosphere, made it so much more traumatic for her when, not very much later, she should be the one to most emphatically shatter the pervading pleasantness.

Having just had to regretfully refuse a second helping of *pesche ripiene*, Jayme was happily sipping her coffee when Enéa Mondadori asked his son if they might use his study after dinner, as he had something he would like to discuss with him.

'This sounds serious, *Padre*,' Nerone replied, and as Jayme took another sip of her coffee she felt the light humour in his voice to be most captivating.

She was abruptly startled out of her pleasant thoughts, however, when in reply his father said, 'I have been giving the matter some thought, and it seems to me to be most important that we look into the position of Jayme's financial security.' Jayme's eyes shot to the senior Mondadori. Scarcely believing her hearing, she clearly heard him add, 'Since Jayme has no father of her own, I should like to make provision for my new daughter.' And, while his words sank in and her pride grew indignant, he went on to ask his son, 'You do not object?'

It was then that Jayme fractured the most agreeable atmosphere. With her pride rocketing, she did not give Nerone time to reply, but bluntly, if politely, she spoke up. 'I object, Signor Mondadori. I'm afraid I object most strongly.'

The hush that fell over the graceful dining-room was one of complete astonishment. At least Jayme was astonished by the happenings of the last minute or so, and Signor and Signora Mondadori, sitting opposite her at the oblong table, both looked startled by her sudden announcement. But as Jayme turned her head slightly it was to see that Nerone, who stared coldly back at her, was the only one who did not appear in any way taken out of his stride. Though, sitting that close to him, she suddenly perceived that there was something in the dark eyes that held hers that was a trifle menacing.

His tone, however, was even when, looking away from her, he addressed his father, and, if she could believe her ears, said lightly, 'My fiancée, I have learned, *Padre*, has a great deal of pride.' Jayme's left hand lay in her lap, and her heart gave a rapid burst of activity when all at once Nerone's right hand caught a warning hold of it beneath the table as he went on, 'Jayme is so used to looking after others that she has difficulty in accepting that someone might find pleasure in looking after her. Is that not so, *cara*?' he enquired, his grip on her hand tightening dangerously.

'I'm . . .' she began defiantly, then looked into his eyes, and suddenly hated him because, loving him, she found it impossible to go against what he said in front of his parents—and she did not like that one tiny bit. She took her glance from him and looked across the table towards his father—and knew no alternative but to tell him quietly, 'I apologise if I've caused you any offence.'

'Your attitude is understandable,' Enéa Mondadori smiled. 'You will forgive me too, eh, if I have offended you?'

Jayme inwardly felt most unhappy, but she found a smile. 'Of course,' she replied, pulling her hand from Nerone's grip, and did not feel any happier when, once everyone had had enough coffee, he went with his father to the study.

She did not see Nerone again that night, nor did she want to. For the look of the thing she stayed and insisted on helping Signora Mondadori clear away. But as soon as the dishwasher was loaded and the kitchen was once more immaculate—the study door being still closed on its two occupants—Jayme decided to go to bed. She had gone along with Nerone this far, but if he attempted to kiss her goodnight in the same way that he had kissed her last night, she was still feeling inwardly angry enough with him to take a kick at his shins.

'Thank you for a superb dinner,' she told his mother, and, after a few more minutes spent chatting, asked, 'Would you mind if I went to bed?'

'You have had a long day with the sightseeing,' the *signora* said sympathetically, her sympathy making Jayme feel dreadful. 'Shall I tell my son goodnight for you?'

'If you would,' Jayme smiled, though she doubted that Nerone would be all that surprised when he came out from the study to find her gone to bed. 'Signor Mondadori too,' she added.

She undressed and got into bed in a rebellious mood. Nerone and his father had been closeted in the study for simply ages. What in creation were they discussing for so long?

The fact that, by the look of it, a lot of what they were discussing had to be her, added resentment to her feeling of rebellion. 'I am not in the habit of lying to my parents', Nerone had once told her—well, she only hoped he stuck to that, because if he insisted on pretending that they were engaged then, from where she saw it, there would be no stopping his father making some financial provision for her!

Jayme had a fretful night. Time and again as she awoke through the night an awesome sort of premonition awoke with her—that premonition being that Nerone had not said anything to his father on the subject of their *not* being engaged.

Why he should want to continue the pretence was a mystery to her to begin with. At first, the part of her that was deeply in love with him knew a moment of sheer unadulterated elation at the thought that perhaps he was insisting on claiming her to be his fiancée because he truly wanted her to be his fiancée. That moment of idiocy did not last long. It did not take long for her to recall that apart from last night's salute in front of his parents, the only time Nerone had kissed her or shown any desire for her was when, by hitting him the way she had, she had driven him to make some retaliation. A moment after that Jayme was remembering how he had only claimed her as his fiancée in order to protect her in the first place.

She drifted off to sleep, only to wake an hour later to take up where her thinking had left off and to wonder—was it out of some sort of chivalry that Nerone was insisting on carrying on with the myth that they were unofficially engaged? It looked like it. With him being determined to take responsibility for her after the accident, and bearing in mind that his mother had not liked the idea at all of her and Nerone living under the same roof unchaperoned, it seemed to Jayme's weary mind that he was keeping on with the farce of their being engaged as more protection. His feeling of responsibility for her had seen him insist, to the point of blackmail, that she stay in his home until her passport was handed in, or arrangements for a new one had been processed, at any rate.

The next time Jayme awakened, dawn was breaking. She knew she would not go back to sleep again. Donning her dressing-gown, she quietly opened the french windows and stepped out on to the terrace. Everywhere was peaceful—she could only wish that it was so within herself.

She had awakened in a disconsolate frame of mind, and as she meandered across the terrace she knew that the root cause of her unhappiness was Nerone. While she loved him—for even if she might not want to, nothing, it seemed, could change that—it nevertheless irked her that if he was still pretending to be engaged to her then his father might well, as he had stated, be on the way to making some financial provision for her.

She sighed, and as more light gathered in the sky she rebelled at the thought that—even though Signor Mondadori might have sufficient wealth and to spare—she should be put in the position she was in. Not that she would touch a penny of his money, though she hoped it would not get that far. The embarrassment of having to. . .

Abruptly, her thoughts broke off. A sound behind her made her swiftly turn round. Ridiculously then, when she had so much else on her mind—as her heartbeats suddenly began to race as her eyes rested on the bare-legged, short-robe-clad, tall figure of Nerone—that her first thought should be one of utter vanity. But it was too late to wish she had paused to pull a comb through her tousled locks before she had left her room.

She saw that Nerone's eyes were resting on her blonde tresses, and as he started to come closer she thought there was the most friendly look in his dark eyes. But the light was not yet so good that she could be certain.

His voice, however, was affable enough as he enquired quietly, 'Could you not sleep, Jayme?'

The very last thing in her mind just then was to give him any idea of the hours of wakefulness he had caused her. But, whether he was feeling friendly or whether he was not, she most certainly was still disturbed at the position he had put her in, too disturbed not to say something short and sharp on that subject.

'Have you told your father that you and I are *not* engaged?' she demanded abruptly, and, regardless of the quality of the light, she could not miss the way any friendliness in him soon departed at her tone.

Ice had swiftly formed in the eyes that moments before had seemed friendly. And his voice, though still quiet, now had an arrogant and authoritative edge to it when he replied aloofly, 'I trust, *signorina*, that you will not embarrass me by making a scene at the breakfast table.'

'*Me*—embarrass *you*?' she hissed, amazed at the nerve of him. And, when his bare shin looked so inviting to her muled foot, only the memory of the way he had previously exacted full retribution for her physical assault prevented her from taking careful aim. 'You're the absolute limit!' she blazed, and, still not certain she wouldn't physically attack him, she went charging past him back to her bedroom.

Swine! she fumed as she bathed and dressed. What sort of an answer was that to her question? She cooled down somewhat as she sat brushing her hair on her dressing-table stool. 'I trust, *signorina*, that you will not embarrass me by making a scene at the breakfast table' was as good a reply in the negative as any other, she supposed. Quite clearly his father still thought them engaged, and Nerone was likely to object if, at the breakfast table, she told him differently.

Well, little did she care how much Nerone Mondadori objected! she fumed as she left her room to go along to the kitchen to give Signora Mondadori a hand. She had no wish to upset either of the senior Mondadoris, but if mention of 'financial provision' was made again, or indeed any reference to her being engaged to their son, then she had reached a stage where if Nerone would not tell them—she would.

Determined that this time her love for Nerone would not weaken her into going along with anything he said, Jayme went into the kitchen to discover that apparently—with all they required prepared and already on the breakfast-room table—they were breakfasting earlier that morning.

The reason for that consequently took from Jayme all thought about the stand she had been going to make. 'I'm sorry I could not tell you last evening that we must have breakfast early today,' Concetta Mondadori apologised to her when all four in the household were seated at the table. 'But it was only when I awoke this morning that Enéa told me he had some important business he had forgotten, but must attend to today.'

'You're—leaving?'

'I'm afraid so. But,' smiled the *signora*, 'we will meet again and get to know each other before the wedding.'

Jayme opened her mouth, then closed it when, with a great deal of charm, Enéa Mondadori turned to her. 'It seems that the advancing years do not come alone. Are you going to forgive me, Jayme, that my failing memory means we have to leave so soon?'

Jayme looked at him, then half turned to the man who sat next to her and who was a lot like his handsome father in looks. 'Of course,' she told Enéa Mondadori, and because looking at Nerone had again weakened her resolve to say something, she did the only thing she could—she smiled.

An hour later, having just been kissed and embraced by his parents, Jayme stood on the drive with Nerone and waved them off. Then, as their car turned at the bottom of the drive and went out of sight, she too turned, and headed back inside the hall.

'You will join me for refreshment on the terrace?' Nerone called after her as she went up the hall in the general direction of her room.

'No, thanks,' she called over her shoulder. 'I've got some tidying up to do.'

As she was a person of neat disposition, her room needed barely any tidying. What did need tidying, though, she thought glumly, was her tangled mind.

How could she love Nerone so, and yet feel so uneasy within herself that she wanted to leave? How could she want to defy him, yet be so much in love with him that part of her wanted to agree with every word he uttered?

Having done all the tidying necessary, Jayme sat on the edge of her newly made bed and wondered briefly about the confusion being in love brought. Quite desperately did she yearn to be out there on the terrace with Nerone, and yet, even though she had had an invitation to join him, some odd quirk in her nature seemed to condemn her to the solitary gloom of her own company.

What happened now—now that his parents had left? she pondered. Did things just revert to 'normal' until she had her new passport and went home? A cold hand clutched her heart at that thought. Oh, dear heaven, what a muddled creature love had made of her! She knew full well that her mother and her sisters were waiting for her, but, just to show how restless she was inwardly, she knew—which had to make her more perverse than ever—that she did not want to go home. She wanted to stay, and never leave Nerone.

At least, that was her thinking at one minute. The next, though, when without so much as a tap on the glass of the french doors they opened and Nerone stepped into her room, Jayme grew confused again.

'This—is tidying up?' he questioned, his expression unsmiling as, observing that she was doing nothing more than sitting on her bed and staring into space, he took a few more steps into the room.

'Come in!' she snapped with tart sarcasm, and saw immediately that that hadn't gone down very well when his eyes narrowed and his jaw jutted at an aggressive angle.

'What's the matter with you?' he gritted, and took a few more strides, till he was standing over her.

'Since you ask . . .?' Jayme began, and moved from her bed in an angry, agitated movement.

Unfortunately, the movement brought her much too close to Nerone for comfort. Urgently, she went to push past him.

'You tried to unleash your anger in a physical way before!' Nerone reminded her harshly, and too late she realised that he must have seen her trying to push past him as an attempt to hit his arm.

But, whatever he believed—and it all happened too quickly for her to have any very coherent thoughts on the matter—as she made an agitated movement which caught her off balance, Nerone took hold of her. And, as soon as he took hold of her, it seemed as though some kind of irresistible electric current passed between them. She felt it, most definitely she felt it. Then suddenly she was in his arms.

'Jayme!' he breathed, and as her heart leapt, a fire burst into flame within her—all before he had done much more than take her in his arms. With Tusco she had been able to keep her head—with Nerone, Jayme at once knew that she stood no chance. She knew then that she was so in love with Nerone that she would deny him nothing.

'Nerone!' she cried in a strangled kind of way, and that was all he waited to hear. In the next second his head came down, and then his lips met hers in the most beautiful kiss she had ever known.

There was a fire burning in him too, she was aware of that. She saw it in his eyes when he broke that beautiful kiss and pulled back to look into her all-giving eyes. *'Cara!'* he cried, and thrilled her to the core when, his arms pulling her even more closely up to him, he moulded his body against hers, then kissed her again.

Time stood still then as with each kiss more and more anguish in her heart was eased. Her arms were up and around his shoulders when she felt his fingers busy at the fastenings of her blouse.

'Nerone!' she sighed his name, and loved him, was in love with him. She wanted him with all her being when he removed her blouse, then traced tender kisses over her shoulders.

She held on to him tightly when his fingers busied themselves at the back of her and he removed her bra. A moment of shyness gripped her when her bra joined her blouse on the floor, and she buried her face in his neck as she sought for a moment of composure.

What composure she found went flying, though, when with gentle, tender caresses, Nerone's hands traced warmly over her back. She clutched at him tightly as he cupped each naked breast in his hands.

'Oh—Nerone,' she whispered shakily, and no longer felt shy when his mouth suddenly captured hers.

How they came to be sitting turned to each other on her bed, she could not remember. Nor could she remember whether Nerone had removed his shirt by himself or whether she had helped him. But the next time he kissed her, she felt his hair-roughened broad chest against the soft contours of her own body, and it was like something she had never experienced in her life.

'I want—to—touch you,' she murmured huskily, and saw Nerone's smile, warm for her as he allowed her fingers to roam his chest.

Then he kissed her, and then, 'I want to look at you.' he breathed hoarsely.

But suddenly as he looked into her eyes, a scarlet burning blush rushed to Jayme's face—and seemed to tranfix him. Then, while she was taking a grip on herself and trying to convince herself that she had no need to be shy at this first ever moment of a man looking at her breasts and the pink peaks of desire he had created—it was all over! Suddenly, abruptly, and to her most humiliating astoundment, it was ended. In one movement, Nerone's arms dropped away from her and he had bent to pick up her blouse and thrust it back to her.

She was still not accepting what her brain was telling her when he commanded her sharply, 'Cover yourself!' and was shrugging swiftly back into his shirt as sudden coldness smote her. Jayme could not have felt more injured than had he brutally slapped her.

It took her but a moment to comprehend that she had in some way just killed the desire she was certain he had had for her. But it took far longer for her to get herself back together again. Nerone had rejected her—and as that truth sank in and she started to shake so that she could not even get her arms into her blouse, all she had working for her was her pride.

'When it comes to furthering one's education in certain areas,' she found something of a voice to address his rigid back as she held her blouse in front of her, 'you're an expert. But one lesson from you is more than sufficient,' she pushed out coldly from stiff lips. She drew a shaky breath, hoped with all she had that he hadn't heard it, and then, still holding that cool note, 'And now perhaps you could ring and enquire if my passport photos are ready.'

Nerone was at his arrogant worst as, turning, he queried aloofly, 'Passport photos?' as though he had forgotten that he himself had escorted her to have them taken.

'That's what I said!' She saw his glance go to her naked shoulders. 'I want to go home!' she snapped agitatedly. The slamming of her bedroom door told her that Nerone couldn't wait to see her gone.

Her feeling of being rejected, and of utter dejection, was complete, though, when, before he could have had time to ring the photographer, she heard the sound of the Ferrari roaring off down the drive. Clearly he was now so keen to be rid of her that he had no intention of wasting time with phone calls, but was already on his way to collect her passport pictures.

A kind of despair hit Jayme then. She donned a fresh blouse and owned that she felt weepy. But she was not surprised about that. In the last half-hour she had experienced a whole gamut of emotions. Nerone had taken her up to the heights, only to coldly let her fall. It would only be surprising, she thought, had she not felt like bursting into tears.

She was dry-eyed, however, as she got out her suitcase and began to pack. She had no very clear idea where she was going, but some inexpensive *pensione* still seemed to be about the best idea.

The way things stood, she was ninety-nine per cent certain that Nerone would raise no objection when, on his return, she told him she was leaving. She swallowed on a dry sob, and knew that, even if on that one per cent chance he again tried to blackmail her into staying, she would still leave. After this morning's happenings, it no longer seemed to matter so much that he might ring her mother and tell her about the accident, or any of the rest of it.

But Nerone would not try to make her stay, Jayme knew that as she fastened her suitcase and decided she would telephone her mother herself once she was settled in her new and, to be hoped, temporary accommodation. She sighed, feeling irked that she had to be dependent on Nerone returning with her passport photographs before she could leave.

Not that she could depart without thanking him for his hospitality, she thought, forced though her thanks might be in the circumstances. But thank him she would—if it killed her!

Jayme sat down in the cream and gold bedroom chair to wait for Nerone to return and was, at first, fumingly rebellious. Because of her love for him, however, her rebellious feelings were doomed not to last. All too soon, as the minutes slowly ticked by, she began to remember some of his more endearing traits. She loved his laughter, his gentleness. She

loved ... Her thoughts suddenly halted and, knowing
that, most probably within the hour, she would be
leaving this villa where Nerone spent some time every
year, she was suddenly in the grip of an urgency to
take a last look round before he came back.

First she went out on to the terrace and, looking
towards the terrace furniture, she pictured him taking
breakfast there, as occasionally they had together
shared breakfast on the terrace.

Next she went to the kitchen. She felt a twinge of
conscience that, with Rosa still away attending to her
sick daughter, Nerone was going to have to look after
himself. He might be brilliant in the boardroom but,
as she well knew, he had no idea in the kitchen.

Deciding to leave the dining-room and the drawing-
room until last, Jayme went along to Nerone's study.
She opened the door and went in, her thoughts of him
tender as she thought of how hard he must work.

He had earned his holiday, she thought lovingly,
and yet, because of her, it had not been much of a
holiday for him. A stray tear came to her eye as she
thought of how, because of her, this holiday where
he had hoped to do some sailing had seen him take
his boat out only once.

She brushed the tear from her eye, swallowed hard
for control, then discovered that she had been looking
at Nerone's desk for about thirty seconds without
taking anything in. Not that she had any intention at
all of prying. Indeed, she was ready to leave the study,
having photographed in her mind's eye the place where
the man she loved was likely to spend a little of his
'holiday' time. But when she was in the act of half
turning round, something on his desk isolated itself
from everything else, and suddenly she stopped dead
in her tracks.

She stood rooted to the spot, her eyes widening. Then, when she was still far from believing it, though she couldn't see why Nerone, an Italian and proud of it, should have a British passport on his desk, she went over and took the passport up. She opened it.

For perhaps a minute, or even two, Jayme was so stunned at finding her lost passport on his desk that nothing of much import entered her head. Then suddenly, as roaring in came the one truth above all others—that Nerone must have lied and lied and lied to her—all hell broke loose in her.

The swine! The diabolical swine! Outraged, Jayme grabbed up her passport and went back to her room for her case. To think she had been going to hang around to thank him for his hospitality!

As though her suitcase weighed nothing, she charged out of the villa and down the drive. To think, she railed as she went, that not so long ago her conscience had pricked her because he was going to have to look after himself when she left! Incensed, she hoped he *starved*!

Furiously she stormed down the hill. My sainted aunt, had she been an idiot! All too clearly Nerone had been in possession of her passport before that morning. Which meant that if the police had brought it to the villa yesterday while they were out, then one or other of his parents would most certainly have mentioned that fact. Which in turn likewise meant that it could not have been delivered to the villa the day before either, or, by the same token, his parents would have mentioned it.

Which left Jayme knowing that Nerone could very possibly have had her passport in his possession for ages—even before he had taken her to have some passport photos taken to facilitate the issue of a new one.

My godfathers, had he taken her for a ride! He'd blackmailed her into the bargain, she fumed, when, sore at heart, she cooled down marginally to realise that she stood every chance of falling over and breaking her neck if she carried on downhill at this pace.

What was it about her, she wondered as she slowed her pace and began to become aware of the weight of her suitcase, that, when she could not abide being lied to, not one Italian male, but two, had led her so easily up the garden path?

Jayme halted her stride and put down her case with the intention of changing it from one hand to the other. Suddenly, though, she realised she had come to a halt right outside the gate of her favourite spot— the public olive grove. The hurt inside her was reaching screaming pitch, and to have so unknowingly stopped at just that place seemed to be an omen. She had found peace and tranquillity in the olive grove before, she recalled, and the next she knew was that, as though compelled, she had opened the gate and was inside, and going over to one of the benches.

Setting her suitcase down on the ground, she sat on the bench and faced the fact that she had no hope of recapturing the feeling of peace and tranquillity she had once known. Then the vague notion started to float around in her head that now she had her passport she could go on down into Torbole and see about hiring a taxi to take her to the airport in Verona.

But, with her emotions churning inside her, she was not capable of acting on vague notions just yet. Any stray thought of Tusco Bianco and the way he had led her on soon went from her mind. Nerone was a better man, and she had not expected *him* to play on her gullibility. She had *trusted* him. Yet he too had lied to her. Dear heaven, she had vowed after Tusco that she would see the lies coming the next time. My stars—she hadn't even ducked!

The hurt Nerone had inflicted was like a raw open wound. Time passed as she bravely delved to discover why he should lie to her like that. Perhaps lying to Englishwomen was the sport of the year for Italian men, she thought at one sour and particularly low point.

She was so involved, though, in trying to fathom just why Nerone should let her believe her passport was still lost, when he had it in his possession, that she did not hear the sound of someone at the olive grove gate. The last time she had been there, she had been aware that she had company when she had heard the gate open. This time she neither heard it open nor close. Nor, some few seconds later, did she hear the sound of nearing footsteps which would have told her that she again had company.

Indeed, so hurt, so taken up with her thoughts was she that she was oblivious to everything in her search for the answer that eluded her, until suddenly a voice she knew and loved asked tautly, 'Are you so unhappy, Jayme, that you have to run away from me?'

Stunned to hear him so unexpectedly, she looked up rapidly. Sea-green eyes met dark eyes, but as her heart began to race and she recognised that there was a grim light in his eyes, she got her second wind and tilted her chin defiantly. She had her passport and could return to England any time she wanted, but if Nerone Mondadori di Vallanetto wanted a fight, by heaven, had he come to the right place!

CHAPTER EIGHT

'UNHAPPY!' Jayme erupted, still metaphorically lacing up her boxing gloves. 'You think I should stay at home meekly waiting . . .' Her voice tailed off and she could have kicked herself for calling his villa 'home'. 'When exactly,' she changed course to question in sharp tones, 'did you find my passport?'

Staring up at Nerone, she did not miss the alert look that entered his eyes. But, when she was sure he must have remembered that he had her passport on the top of his desk and that, with his intelligence, he would have quickly realised she had seen it, her anger went soaring as he questioned in reply, 'Passport?' and seemed to her to be playing for time.

Glaring at him furiously, Jayme wanted to hit him and hit him again. For, like Tusco, he was a liar and, like Tusco, he was an actor, and in her heart she wept because she had thought and believed him all that Tusco Bianco was not.

'Yes, passport,' she snapped hotly. 'The one, the British one, which you left lying around on your desk. Rather careless of you, wouldn't you say?' she hissed aggressively.

For long, ageless moments, Nerone looked into her angry sparking eyes. But, when she would not have put it past him to have the nerve to enquire what she was doing in his study in the first place, he merely murmured an even, 'I see,' and—which was no help whatsoever to her inner agitation—moved his long length and came and sat down beside her on the bench.

'I'm glad you do,' she told him hostilely, and stared determinedly in front of her.

Her agitation went up by many degrees, however, when all at once gentle but firm hands took her shoulders, and Nerone turned her so that he could see into her face. It was instinctive in her to want to turn to face the front again, but, when his hands left her shoulders, Jayme was of the opinion that maybe, rather than risk those tingling sensations he aroused in her so effortlessly should he again take hold of her, she would stay turned the way she was. She would be going on her way soon, anyhow, she determined stoutly.

'You've every right to be angry, Jayme,' Nerone told her when with warring eyes she stared at him.

'Generous to a fault!' she flared belligerently, but his touch had already weakened her, and in the face of his eyes holding hers unwaveringly she was having the greatest difficulty in maintaining an antagonistic attitude. 'When,' she fired, grabbing at what acid she could, 'did you find it—and don't tell me this morning, because...'

Her voice faded when, not a bit angered by her bossy manner, it seemed, Nerone quietly broke in, 'Your passport, my dear, was never lost.'

Jayme's mouth fell open—she quickly closed it. His English 'my dear' had sounded warm and wonderful in her ears—but quickly she pulled herself back together. There were more important issues at stake here than for her to be sidetracked by any throwaway endearment he might care to use. 'M-my passport— was n-never lost?' she spluttered. Witlessly she stared at him for a moment, then, 'Is that the truth?' she heard herself question feebly. But that was before she brought herself up smartly, and realised he wouldn't recognise truth if it rose up and bit him. 'You liar!' she raged. 'You treacherous, lying...'

'Calm yourself, Jayme, calm yourself,' Nerone came in swiftly. 'I agree I've evaded the truth a little...'

'A *little*!' she flared.

'However, I'm not sure that I'd agree that I've acted treacherously towards you.'

'You don't call blackmail treachery? You don't call conning me into believing I had to stay in Italy until either my passport was handed in to the police or...' abruptly she broke off. 'You rang the police. I was there the day you did it,' she remembered. 'Aren't there laws in this country against people who waste police time?'

'I'm sure there most probably are,' he agreed. 'But to waste police time is one crime which, since I've known you, I have not committed.'

By the sound of it, he was saying that he had only turned to crime since he had known her. But Jayme did not thank him, either for that implication, or for the fact that he was *blatantly* still lying now!

'Yes, you did!' She refused to allow him to get away with it. 'You rang the police in both Verona and Torbole—I heard you!'

'Forgive me,' Nerone answered calmly, and caused her jaw to drop again as he went on, 'but the two numbers I rang that day were both numbers chosen at random. One did not answer, the other gave the engaged signal.'

Jayme stared at him disbelievingly. 'You rang...
You spoke to—the ringing-out tone? You made an
enquiry about my passport to the engaged tone!' she
exclaimed, her voice rising.

'*Si,*' Nerone replied, and Jayme's pugilistic tend-
encies awakened with a vengeance.

'You rat!' she snapped. 'You diabolical,
loathsome...' Words failed her. But, afraid she might
yet start physically lashing out, she jumped hastily to
her feet. She was leaving. She'd heard enough—more
than enough!

She bent to pick up her case, and in the same
movement went to take an angry step away from him.
Which was when Nerone, rapidly on his feet too,
caught hold of her arm.

'Take your hand off me!' she shrieked. Already off
balance, but with her suitcase in her grip, she was
furious enough to let him feel the full weight of it.
Enraged, she swung it at him—only to find that he
had, with an amazing speed, taken it from her, and
to discover that she was seated back on the bench.

Feeling slightly winded, Jayme was staring at him
when something Italian, and in the nature of a swear
word, she imagined, escaped him. Then, as though
to watch that *she* did not escape, he blocked part of
her path with her suitcase, and seated himself closer
to her this time than before. 'To use your expression,
Jayme,' he commented, 'grief, what a temper! You're
quite dangerous when roused, little one.'

'You should be boiled in oil!' she fumed, starting
to feel a little ashamed that but a few moments ago
she had so far lost control as to be furious enough to
happily want to hit him with her heavy case!

'You're very likely correct about that,' he murmured. 'But...' He hesitated, and as she stared hostilely at him, Jayme was not certain that, for the only time since she had known him, he did not appear to be a little unsure of his ground.

'But what?' she asked. Though her tone was short, she still wanted to bite her tongue out that part of her should still wish to help him out.

'But there is a reason for everything that I have done since knowing you.'

There it was again—that implication that seemed to state that only since he had met her had he turned into the lying devil she now knew him to be. 'I'll bet there is!' she snapped waspishly, and as far as she was concerned had given him all the encouragement she was going to in her previous 'But what?'

'Do you not want to hear anything of that reason, Jayme?' Nerone asked seriously, his eyes intent on hers.

'To hear more of your lies, you mean?' she blazed. 'To hear you amuse yourself at my expense with yet more...'

'No!' he cut in sharply, and looked angry for the first time since he had entered the olive grove. 'I never have amused myself at your expense,' he grated harshly. 'I've too much—regard—for you for that!'

Foolishly, her heart leapt—oh, how she wanted his regard! But what she did not want were lies—especially from him. 'Are you saying you've turned over a new leaf?' she enquired with her best sarcasm.

'I'm saying that all falsehoods of the past are done,' he stared solemnly into the sceptical depths of her seagreen eyes to state. 'I'm saying that, regardless of what cost to myself, and to my pride, I shall speak only the truth to you from now on.'

How sincere he sounds, she thought, and was hard put to it not to swallow on a knot of emotion. 'You're trying to tell me that you've lied to me because of your pride?' Jayme, who had pride herself, and then some, attempted to work it out. 'You're saying that...' she paused in her search for comprehension '...that...' She broke off again. She felt confused, and just couldn't fathom what Nerone was or was not saying. 'This sounds—er—of some—er—consequence,' she said quietly, and coughed to clear a constriction in her throat.

'It is,' Nerone replied, 'of great consequence.' Warily she eyed him. 'Don't be afraid, Jayme,' he quickly told her. 'If you've learned nothing more of me in our time together, then I hope at least you've learned that I would never harm you.'

Again she was struck by his sincerity. But he had lied to her, and she—she hated lies. 'I've learned that you're capable of confiscating my passport and have then gone to extraordinary lengths to pretend to me that it was lost.' Jayme fought hard against believing in his sincerity—and won.

'I can explain—if you'll permit me,' Nerone returned harshly.

'So,' she snapped, 'suppose you start speaking "only the truth"? How about beginning by telling me how my passport got from my possession into yours?' she challenged, and as the thought struck, 'You didn't rifle in my shoulder bag to...!'

'Of course I didn't!' he interrupted sharply, and was all arrogant proud Italian as, prefixing his comment with what she thought was another Italian swearword, 'What kind of man do you think I am?' he snarled.

He was the kind of man she had fallen in love with, but she would cut her tongue out sooner than let him know it. And she'd be damned if she'd apologise for offending him, either. 'Well, if you didn't take it from my bag, I don't know how else you got hold of it!' she hurled at him unrepentantly. 'It was in my bag the last time I...'

'It fell from your bag!' Nerone cut her off, obviously still angry with her.

'When?' she tilted her chin to demand.

'If you'll be quiet for a moment, I'll tell you!' he thundered. She opened her mouth to tell him to stop ordering her about, then closed it again. Nerone waited only a moment to see that it did not look as though she had anything more to add, and then, his tone evening out, he enlightened her. 'It was the day of our meeting.'

'That far back!' she gasped, and received an exasperated look from him for her trouble. For the moment she forbore to add anything.

'I'd just caught you a glancing blow with my car,' Nerone went on after again satisfying himself that she would stay quiet for a few seconds. 'You had fainted and were dead to the world.' A haunted kind of look came into his eyes and, had she not known better, Jayme would have thought that that moment of seeing her lifeless had haunted him many times since.

'You thought I was dead?' she questioned, as the honesty in her soul made her admit that if the circumstances were reversed that she would be haunted too if she ever knocked anyone over, regardless of where the blame lay.

'No,' he denied. 'But at that moment I'd no idea of the extent of your injuries.'

'You took me to... You brought me in here to find out?' she questioned, and knew she had got it wrong when he shook his head.

'I brought you here to recover,' he informed her, and as she realised that of course no one moved an injured person until one was sure that the casualty didn't have a broken back or something, he went on, 'But, with you unconscious and with your belongings scattered on a busy thoroughfare, I had to move fast.'

'My bag had come open as it hit the ground?' she worked out, and saw him nod.

'I brought you in here and then hurried to retrieve your case and your bag from the road,' he told her. 'In my efforts to avoid running you down, though, I'd slewed my car across the road. If there was not to be another accident around these blind corners, I realised I'd have to take time and drive my car out of the way of other traffic.'

This was the first time Jayme had heard any of this, and her admiration for Nerone went up in leaps and bounds as she forgot all about his underhandedness about her passport.

'It all sounds a bit hairy!' she could not help exclaiming.

'It was,' he told her with a hint of a smile, and it was he who reminded her of what all this was about when he went on, 'I didn't notice your passport until after I'd moved my car.' He shrugged. 'With such an important document, I had to spare another few seconds from you to collect it and put it in my car for safekeeping.'

Jayme could do nothing to stop the wild flutter of her heart. Nerone had said that as though he meant he could not bear to be away from her for a second. Again, though, she brought herself up short. When was she going to learn, for goodness' sake? Didn't she know already that he could lie through his back teeth? Was she now going to take as gospel every word he said—take his every intonation as meaning more than, on the face of it, it did?

'So, having got hold of my passport, you thought it would be good sport to lead me on when I told you I'd lost it!' she came out of her compliant state to fire.

'Nothing of the sort!' Nerone exploded angrily, no hint of a smile about him then.

'Huh!' Jayme scorned. 'You'd every intention of returning it to me, I suppose?' she enquired sarcastically, and heard from the hiss of his harsh indrawn breath that her opposition was making him more angry than ever—and that suited her just fine.

'Damn you, *signorina*!' he snarled. 'I did have every such intention!'

'Why didn't you, then?' she charged, sparks again flashing from her eyes.

'Because . . .' he started to hurl, then stopped. Then he looked into her angry, challenging face. 'Is it any wonder that I've come near to losing my reason?' he growled.

'Whatever that might mean,' Jayme responded acidly, 'I'm sure I'm going to get the blame!'

For an age Nerone continued to look at her, but made no comment. Then suddenly every vestige of anger seemed to drain from him, and he asked, 'Can you not give a little, Jayme?'

Again her heartbeat gained speed. While Nerone stayed angry, she thought she could match him. But that he should ask something of her in a gentler tone was weakening, and she had nothing to meet it with. Be fair, Nerone, she wanted to tell him. Play fair, she wanted to say. But she could not, and knew she could not, for to do so would reveal the power he had over her. And, whatever else he might know, he must never know that she was in love with him.

'Of course,' she told him brightly. 'What would you like me to give—more of my gullibility? More of my naïve credulity? More of...'

'I've told you,' he cut harshly in through her sarcasm, 'that never again will I lie to you!'

'That's right—you won't!' she stormed, but, when she would have again attempted to leave, Nerone's hand, as though he had anticipated her move, was there to prevent her from going anywhere. And she realised he was angry—more angry than ever!

'You will hear me out, *signorina*!' he thundered. 'If I have to tie you to this bench, you'll hear me out!'

Jayme looked into the burning fierceness of his eyes, and didn't doubt that he meant it. Though why he should threaten such desperate action defeated her. Defeated and, she had to own, intrigued her.

'That—er—sounds a bit—um—drastic,' she murmured.

'Can you wonder?' he questioned shortly. 'You, *signorina* are driving me to distraction!'

Amazed by what he had just said, she stared at him. But when this time she searched for sarcasm, there was none to be found, and when she did find her voice, to her horror, it sounded more trusting than sarcastic as she enquired quietly, 'That's why you stole my passport, is it?'

Again Nerone looked at her for long moments. But although he appeared far from relaxed, her tone seemed to have caused his anger to depart abruptly. His voice was without heat too, as he told her quietly, 'I didn't mean to steal it, or to hang on to it. With so much else on my mind, I'd even forgotten that I had it until you came and told me that you'd lost it.'

Jayme had no idea what he meant by 'With so much else on my mind', but since she had only recently decided that she was not going to read meanings into everything he said that just weren't there, she took his remarks at face value. Clearly his head was busy with work even when he was on holiday.

'You remembered, though, that you had it when I mentioned its loss?' she remained quiet and calm to question.

'*Si.*' He nodded. 'I'd transferred it from my car to my desk drawer for continued safekeeping.' He broke off, then went on, though more slowly this time, 'I had every intention of returning it to you. Before I could do so, however, to my amazement, when it was clear to me you were having difficulty remaining vertical and should still be in your bed, you came looking for me to tell me you wanted to return to England.'

'Yes, well, you'd been more than kind as it was,' she explained. 'I didn't want to trespass on your hospitality any...'

'Trespass on my hospitality!' Nerone cut in, clearly astounded that she could even think such a thing. 'Don't you know that you could never do that?'

'I—er...' Jayme faltered, and found she was confessing, 'You didn't seem to like it when you realised from that first telephone call I made to England that I knew someone in Italy. I felt then that you'd rather I went and—er—recuperated with the other person I knew.'

'Never!' he roared vehemently, going on explosively, 'What the hell gave you the impression that I'd let you go to Bianco? I would *never* have allowed you to go to him!' he told her in no uncertain terms. 'Never!'

'Well, I didn't—I . . .' His anger, his vehemence left her stuck for words. 'But . . .' Feeling totally confused, she broke off, and stared helplessly at him. 'I wouldn't have gone to Tusco anyway,' she told him as she suddenly remembered how, regardless of the falsehoods Nerone had allowed her to believe, he had been totally on her side when it came to protecting her, and her pride, from Tusco Bianco. 'I told you at the time that I was leaving Italy that day—only I'd lost my passport.'

'So you did,' Nerone replied, then went on to astonish her when, his anger and vehemence all at once evaporated, he quietly added, 'And I realised that I was prepared to do anything—to keep you in Italy.' Her eyes were saucer-wide as he tacked on, 'Even if it meant I should have to hold on to your passport.'

'You . . .' Jayme tried. 'You . . .' she tried again, and was still staring at him disbelievingly when she at last managed to string a sentence together. 'You didn't want m-me to leave? You—you deliberately hung on to my passport . . .'

'I hadn't meant to,' he owned, his eyes steady on her still incredulous ones. 'I even hesitated,' he went on, then told her, 'Then I knew that it was the only way.'

Stunned, Jayme sat and stared at him. Then suddenly she began to grow wary. Why was it the only way? Way for what? Why? the question spun round in her brain. Why would he go to the extent of pretending to phone the police to fool her into believing he had no knowledge of her passport? Why? For goodness' sake, he had even taken her to the photographer's to have some passport photos taken in his attempt to keep up the charade that her passport was well and truly lost!

Jayme looked away from him for a second or two as she tried to get her thoughts together. But with no answers arriving, her faith in him was too badly shattered for her to feel able to risk asking him the pointblank question 'why?' On present evidence, though, despite his assurance that he would speak only the truth from now on, she felt it would do no harm to continue to be chary of him.

'You—er—seem to have wanted me to stay quite badly?' she flicked her glance back to his good-looking face to query.

'I did,' he confirmed, which, she thought, told her very little.

'To the—er—extent of lying to me?' she questioned, a coolness starting to enter her tone once more.

'I confess it, Jayme,' Nerone owned. 'Much as I did not want to lie to you, I found it necessary to lie— either by deliberately allowing you to draw the wrong inference, or by telling you an outright lie.'

Had she not loved him so very much, Jayme felt she would then have made a more determined effort to be on her way. But because she loved him so much and wanted to be in possession of the full facts when she returned to England, something in her made her more determined to stay and hear everything there was to hear. As yet, though, why Nerone had found it *necessary* to lie was still a mystery to her.

'You've told other lies?' she asked carefully. 'Besides the...' was it inference or outright lie about her passport? She couldn't remember '...the one about my passport?' she questioned.

'I lied to you when I told you that Rosa had been summoned urgently to go and nurse her sick daughter. I...'

'Rosa's daughter wasn't ill?' Jayme enquired, and was startled anew when Nerone replied,

'She hasn't got a daughter.'

'She hasn't...! But...' Jayme gasped.

'Forgive me,' he said quietly, as his eyes scrutinised her staggered expression. 'I wanted you here with me, as I've told you. But, in the short while that I'd known you, I had realised several things.'

'You—had?' she queried cautiously.

'Oh, but yes,' he answered gently. 'You not only have a natural beauty of face and body, you have a natural beauty of mind too. You have pride, you have courage and, I was beginning to discover, you have a softness of heart when you know you are needed. As I've said, I wanted you to stay with me but, having seen you proud in your statement that you would leave, I realised that I'd only get you to stay if I could convince you that you were needed—here.'

'Ah,' said Jayme as the penny began to drop. 'You sent Rosa away and...'

'I told Rosa that she needed a holiday and drove her to stay with her sister, then drove like fury back to my villa, fearing quite desperately that you might be gone before I could get back to you.'

Jayme's head was abuzz with what he was telling her. Intertwined with his revelation about telling Rosa she needed a holiday was a memory of him telling his mother that Rosa was on holiday. At that point Jayme saw how completely duped she had been.

'You're not helpless in the kitchen at all, are you?' she questioned him stonily.

'To quite some degree, I am,' he replied, her changing tone seeming to bother him somewhat, for he was frowning as, truthfully, he now owned, 'But I'm not as helpless as I pretended when I wanted you to see how very much I needed a housekeeper.'

'Why?' Jayme charged bluntly.

'Why did I need a housekeeper?' he asked in return, and seemed so genuinely not to understand what she was asking that Jayme, in a sudden flurry of anger, could have hit him.

'Why,' she said tartly, 'have you gone to the lengths you have to keep me here? Why the lies about Rosa, about my passport? Why—any of it?' she questioned irately, and even waved an angry hand in the air.

It was that hand which Nerone caught and held, and suddenly Jayme was suffering emotions other than anger. With a show of outward calm, however, she tried to wrest her hand from him—but he would not let it go.

Glaring at him, she saw that his expression was never more serious. But she was looking at him more poleaxed than glaring, when suddenly he murmured, 'Jayme, my stubborn, proud darling, can you not open your ears and your heart to all that I've been trying to tell you?'

Her heart at once set up a commotion within her. Her eyes were wide and fixed on him as, without success, she tried to answer him. 'I . . .' she began.

'Don't you know, *mia cara,*' he went on, seeing she was lost for words, 'that I was so afraid that if you went to England you might not be willing to see me when I followed you that I had to keep you here.'

'You . . .' she said hoarsely, 'you—would have followed me to England?'

'England—anywhere,' he answered solemnly, and Jayme started to tremble.

'Why—would you have d-done that?' she asked in a strangled voice that sounded like anybody's but her own.

If she was feeling under something of a strain, however, Nerone, she saw, looked as if he might suddenly break from strain when, after long, long moments of staring into her face, 'For love,' he quietly replied. 'For love, Jayme.'

'For—love!' she echoed on a whisper of sound, and felt all over the place as Nerone took her other hand in a firm grip.

As if needing something to steady himself, he held fast on to her two hands, then, taking a deep breath, he said deep in his throat, 'For love—of you—dearest Jayme.'

She gave an instinctive pull, but her hands stayed firmly in his clasp. She looked away from his sincere dark eyes, then back again. She wanted to believe the truth and honesty she saw in the steady gaze that looked straight back. Then she remembered what he had said earlier—that, regardless of cost to himself and to his pride, he would speak only the truth from now on. He was a proud man, she knew that. Was he saying that, because he had no idea how she felt about him, he was risking his pride by telling her of his love? She did not know what to believe any more. She had trusted her instincts before and had been wrong. Nerone had implied things before, and she had made up the rest—and been wrong.

'Oh, Nerone!' she wailed agitatedly.

She saw him swallow, and felt his grip on her hands tighten. 'Does that mean that you care, or does it mean that, with your so tender heart, you do not care but don't wish to wound me by telling me that you cannot care?' he asked gruffly.

'It means—that—I don't know what to believe!' she cried.

'Then you care—you must care!' he exclaimed, and appeared then as though he might have taken her jubilantly in his arms. But suddenly he seemed to recognise from her anxious, large-eyed look that he would have to tell her more if she was to be convinced. 'Perhaps it will help you to believe, Jayme,' he said quietly, keeping a firm hold on her hands but making no closer movement than that, 'if I tell you how—from the moment I first saw you—life for me changed.'

'H-how?' Jayme found her voice to choke.

'You stepped out in front of my car, and even now I go cold when I remember it,' he replied. 'Thank heaven I wasn't driving fast! I knew at once that I couldn't avoid hitting you, so was it any wonder that my heart should suddenly pound?'

'I—suppose not,' Jayme murmured.

'The staggering thing, though,' Nerone continued, 'was that even when I was certain I had done you no permanent injury, my heart was still pounding.'

'You'd—had a—scare,' she reminded him, and he looked gently at her.

'I'd fallen in love—at first sight, *cara*,' he told her tenderly. 'I'd waited for you all my life, and I knew you were the one, before you had so much as opened your eyes.'

Jayme swallowed, and tried her hardest to be sensible. But with her heart racing inside her, her voice was not disbelieving, but husky with emotion, as she asked, 'Is—that true?'

'I swear it,' he replied fervently.

'Oh!' she mumbled, loving his look of sincerity, but still afraid to trust.

But it seemed Nerone was prepared to stay talking to her for as long as it took to convince her of his sincerity, and convince her that she could trust him, for he was going on, 'I feared I'd hurt you more than I'd realised when you were shaky and light-headed and near to fainting again. But your shakiness after the accident worked in my favour, because I then had the marvellous opportunity of taking you to my holiday home.'

'That pleased you?' she questioned.

'Of course,' he replied promptly, though he qualified, 'Naturally my initial anxiety about you was such that I summoned a doctor without delay.' He paused, then confessed, 'It was then—that my lies began.'

'Oh,' Jayme murmured, and then, despite her stubborn unwillingness to believe another lying word, 'How? When?' she invited.

'The very next day,' he did not hesitate to tell her. 'You were still far from well and suffering a reaction of fatigue, yet there you were saying that you would leave your bed.' There was a trace of a smile about his mouth as he informed her, 'It seemed to me, *cara*, that the next I should hear was that you had decided to leave me. I most certainly could not have that, though I feel I may have stretched the truth of Dr Prandelli's instructions a little too far when I let you believe you must either rest in bed or hospital.'

She stared at him, her mouth open. Hurriedly she closed it. 'He—didn't say anything of the kind?'

He shook his head. 'For fear he might show me up for a liar, I had to get him from your room quickly after his second visit.'

'Good heavens!' she exclaimed faintly, and could not but soften towards Nerone when his superb smile flashed out, and he said,

'I had you in my home, my dear; I'd no intention that you should leave. I was in love with you, and I wanted you where I could be with you the whole of the time.'

'You—did?' she murmured softly.

'Oh, so much, beautiful Jayme,' he breathed. 'I was more and more under the spell of you as each minute passed. I heard you laugh, and was enchanted. I'd seen your loyalty to your family when, wanting to know everything about you, I discovered how you'd sacrificed full-time education to help them.'

'It wasn't as dramatic as that,' she interrupted.

'You're doing it again—being loyal to your family,' Nerone said. 'Can you wonder that, when I was already in love with you, I began to admire every selfless trait about you?'

'Oh, don't, Nerone—I'm not that good,' she denied, and saw from his expression that he did not believe her for a moment.

'Can you wonder that I was afraid to let you go for fear you would refuse to see me when I pursued you to England? But,' he went on, 'while I was still desperately trying to work out ways of keeping you in Italy so I could pay my court to you, I was totally furious to overhear—in your telephone call to your mother—that there was another man in your life!'

'Is *that* why you were so furious?' Jayme gasped.

'Never have I known such savage jealousy,' Nerone owned. 'I was incensed that, while I was biding my time until you were well enough for me to begin my courtship, there were you talking of marriage—to someone else! It was more than I could take!'

'But...' Jayme began as she remembered his fury at the time, then, as what he had just said separated itself from everything else, she forgot completely what she had been going to say, and said instead, 'Marriage? Are—you—talking of...' Suddenly, as her heart started to pound more than ever, she was just incapable of saying another word.

But not so Nerone. 'I'm talking of marriage, *amore mia*,' he breathed. 'Me—to you.'

'Oh!' Jayme cried shakily, and was enraptured—for all of five seconds. Then she remembered—she had been this way before. Ice abruptly entered her heart.

'What is it, *cara*?' Nerone asked urgently, when the change that came over her expression betrayed that she was no longer prepared to hear him out.

'What should be the matter?' she asked him through stiff lips. 'It's my experience that Italian men speak easily of marriage without having any intention of fulfilling that promise!' She had come to a biting end, but saw at once that if she was angry, then she had made Nerone instantly, absolutely furious.

'How dare you?' he demanded fiercely, and was so outraged that he flung her hands from him. 'How dare you speak of me and that reptile Bianco in the same breath? You...'

'How dare I?' Jayme blazed, having once been taken for a fool but renewing her determination that it was never going to happen again. 'You're saying that you're different?' she challenged hotly. 'You're saying that you don't tell lies? You're saying that you haven't been playing a part all along? That you haven't been acting a role all these weeks with the sole intention of...' Suddenly she ran out of steam. 'Of...' she tried to carry on, but it was no use.

But that was when she found that Nerone was insisting that she carry on. 'Finish it!' he commanded her curtly. 'Finish what you were saying, *signorina*!' he charged her arctically.

'Oh, Nerone,' she said hopelessly, 'you know—I can't.'

Bluntly she realised that he could. 'How dare you put me in the same honourless class as your former man friend?' he charged. 'How dare you accuse me of only pretending to want to marry you in order to get you into bed? How dare you,' he went on, chips of ice in the eyes that glared at her, 'when you have evidence of how I've denied my desire for you? When you know full well that had my sole aim been to satiate lust for your body, I could have done so this very morning!'

Nerone had come to a cutting and a truthful end. For Jayme could not deny that, had he not been the one to call a halt to their lovemaking that morning, then most certainly she herself would not have done so.

Suddenly it was as though the scales of her obstinate refusal to see the truth, to believe the truth, had dropped from her eyes. Suddenly she had no need to question why he had slammed out from her room that morning. He had wanted her, but to prove his love—maybe to prove that all men were not like Tusco Bianco—he had, while wanting her, realised that he must not take that which she would freely have given.

Which, Jayme all at once realised as joy burst into her heart, meant that Nerone did want to marry her and that he did truly love her.

Her colour was high as, looking unwaveringly into his hostile expression, she said softly, 'Nerone, will you forgive me?'

For several seconds, as her heart beat painfully within her, and he, all proud Italian, looked coldly back at her, she thought he was going to ignore her question. Or, worse, that he would get up and leave her. Then suddenly she thought she perceived a slight thawing in his expression—a slight, very slight hint of an upward curve touch the corners of his mouth.

'If you marry me,' he said crisply, 'I might.'

'Oh, Nerone,' she sighed, 'I do love you!'

The next she knew was that she was in Nerone's arms. 'I knew it! I knew it!' he cried exultantly. 'Oh, my dear, my dear,' he breathed, and buried his face in her neck. 'For all my fear that I might be wrong, something deep down—something in my knowledge of you—insisted that you could not be the responsive, giving woman you've been in my arms and not care. Not you, *cara*, my chaste virgin.' He pulled back from her to look adoringly into her eyes. 'Oh, *mia adorabile*!' he cried, and kissed her.

Time stood still for a little while as Jayme returned Nerone's kisses, and rejoiced in the true knowledge that he loved her. And, when it seemed that he would never have enough of her kisses—and she certainly felt the same way about *his*—he kissed her some more. Then, gently, he was putting her away from him—or at least, while keeping hold of her, he was putting some daylight between their two bodies.

'*Cara,*' he said tenderly. Then, with an attempt at humour, 'I'm merely mortal,' he reminded her.

'I—er—know,' she said huskily, desiring him as he clearly desired her.

Then suddenly, as if he was still unsure of her, 'You do love me, Jayme?' he questioned, his eyes adoring on her pinkened skin.

'I never knew what love was until I realised I was in love with you,' she told him honestly.

'You didn't love Bianco the same way you love me?' he questioned jealously.

'Now that I know what being truly in love feels like, I know I didn't love him at all,' she smiled, and to her joy Nerone, breathing words of endearment in Italian and in English, tenderly kissed her.

'How long?' he then wanted to know. 'How long have you known that you loved me? When did it start?' he asked. 'When...?' He broke off, then grinned the most endearing grin. 'I've been patient for so long; can you wonder that I'm impatient to know everything in two minutes?'

This time Jayme tenderly kissed him. 'I love you, darling Nerone,' she whispered shyly. 'And I've known the depth of my feelings for a couple of days now. Since, in fact, you kissed me goodnight when we came back from Venice. I—just knew then,' she smiled.

'Then it *was* shyness which made you put the barrier of a tray between us when I would have kissed you good morning yesterday!' he exclaimed, and, not waiting for her answer, 'Have you any idea of the hell I've been in, wondering if it was shyness or if you really did have an aversion to my kisses?' he asked.

'I've no aversion to your kisses,' Jayme told him happily, 'none whatsoever. Yesterday, though, I was afraid of giving away the fact that I'd fallen in love with you.'

'Sweet love,' he breathed. 'Thank heaven you were not afraid to tell me today!' Gently he kissed her again, then asked, 'When did it start—this love you have for me?'

'I'm not certain,' she owned. 'Though from the very beginning, when it seemed my world was falling apart, I've felt comforted, secure somehow, to feel the touch of your hand.'

'Ah,' Nerone smiled. 'Did you know that, the first day you were in my home, you went to sleep holding my hand?'

'Did I?'

He nodded. 'You refused to let go of it, too, until Dr Prandelli arrived and I had to wake you.'

'I'm sorry,' she murmured, and was delighted to see him grin again.

'Don't be. It was one of the better moments for me.'

'Has it been that bad—loving me?' she questioned softly.

'Pure hell,' he smiled. 'There am I, in love with this most beautiful woman, only to discover very soon that she loves elsewhere. What can I do, my heart, but take every care that she does not know of my love?'

'I'm sorry,' Jayme murmured again, and was taken gently into his arms.

He had pulled her head to rest in his shoulder when he told her, 'There were some small consolations on the way,' and she heard the smile in his voice.

'There were?'

'You'd said that there was little point in you loving Bianco, and—since I had no intention that you should marry anyone but me—I agreed. Then there were times, little love, when I so longed to take you in my arms that, regardless that you might think me rude, I had to quickly go from you. One day in particular, I remember, I'd made you so angry that you demanded to know "What the *hell* do you think I am?", and I was so afraid that I might slip up and tell you "The woman of my dreams" that I had to go quickly.'

'I remember that incident!' Jayme said in wonder, having had no idea of the feelings and emotions that must have warred in Nerone that day.

'Yet,' he went on to confess, 'there were times when being apart from you was so unbearable that I had to come looking for you.'

'Was one of those times when I went shopping and you saw me having coffee with Tusco?'

'*Si,*' Nerone grunted. 'I'd planned, when I saw you, to pretend that I'd come to help you carry your shopping. *That* went completely out of my head when I discovered that not only are you having coffee with this other man, but you are *holding hands* with him! Can you wonder that I went insane with jealousy?'

'Oh, Nerone!' Jayme cried. 'I'd merely put my hand out to shake his in final parting. He hung on to it and...' Her voice faded. 'You were furious,' she remembered. 'You claimed me as your fiancée...'

'And a short while later you asked me if I'd gone stark, staring mad, and I, *cara*, thought in my insane jealousy that maybe I had.'

'Because you'd told him...'

'I regretted none of what I'd said when my fury had cooled,' Nerone interrupted. 'I wanted you as my fiancée—even more as my wife.' Jayme was still thrilling from the sound of those last two words when he added, 'But by then you had hit me and I had kissed you and had learned to my great joy that, whether you yet knew it or not, you did not love this other man as much as you thought you did.'

'Because of the—er—way I responded to you?'

'Yes, my love,' he confirmed. 'I had to leave you while I still could, yet I ached to take you in my arms again—though this time to hold you protectively—when the next time I saw you your face was scorched with colour.'

'Instead,' she recalled, 'you were a sarcastic pig.'

'And you paid me out,' he laughed, 'by telling me you had decided to leave.'

'But only to be blackmailed by you for my sins,' she smiled, and asked, 'Would you really have telephoned my mother to tell her the "true version" of what had happened to me?'

'Don't ask,' he replied. 'I've done so many things, said so many things which, before knowing you, I'd have sworn I was incapable of doing.'

'Like lying through your teeth when you told me you'd been in touch with the Embassy about my passport?' she teased.

'That, for one,' he agreed. 'For another, and to gain more time with you, I planted the idea in your soft heart that my mother underwent major surgery last year—when it was minor surgery only.'

'Really?' Jayme gasped. 'You wretch!' she berated him lovingly, then questioned, 'To gain more time with me?'

'My mother, though loving me, my heart, has a very strong sense of right and wrong. Should you tell her a word about your lost passport, or about the true situation between us, then I could not be certain she would not feel it her duty, in the absence of your mother, to take over your protection and your safe return to England.'

'But you lied to her once, wouldn't you have . . .'

'I never lied to her,' he denied.

'But, Nerone, you let her think we were engaged?'

'In my mind, we were engaged.'

'Oh,' Jayme murmured. 'You actually told her our engagement was not official yet,' she pursued the matter.

'It wasn't—was it?' he replied, and she just had to laugh—and was soundly kissed, purely because Nerone could not resist it.

'Er . . .' she began when she had some breath back. 'Um . . .' she tried again when nothing very sensible popped into her head. 'Did you never lie to your father either?' she queried.

'To my father,' Nerone replied, 'I last night confessed everything.'

'Everything?' she queried in astonishment. 'That we weren't really engaged, do you mean?' she asked, pulling away to look at him with saucer-wide eyes.

'Little love,' Nerone breathed tenderly, 'apart from those moments which are intimate between just you and me, my father knows everything there is to know. I've told him how I came to my villa with the idea of having a break from work and of maybe doing some sailing, but how all thoughts of sailing went out of my head when I met you.'

'Really?' she questioned, and he nodded.

'Really,' he smiled, 'but for one day when I made it as far as my boat and so wanted to be back with you that I turned around and came home.'

'Oh, Nerone!' she sighed blissfully.

'When my father realised my great love for you and some of the problems I had in pursuit of my happiness with you, he thought that perhaps I might be able to resolve some of my problems if he and my mother were elsewhere.'

'Heavens!' Jayme gasped. 'Is that the real reason why they left this morning?'

'Of course,' Nerone grinned. 'Though I doubt my mother will hear of it until I contact my father to tell him that all our problems have been resolved.'

'Men!' Jayme said lovingly, and then murmured, 'I wonder how much longer we would have gone on loving each other, yet not knowing it, if I hadn't found my passport and realised . . .'

'Not for much longer, my dear one,' Nerone butted in gently. 'A man can take only so much,' he added, and went on, 'I'm glad now that, having taken your passport from my desk drawer for my father to copy the correct spelling of your name, when he put it back on my desk I did not return it to the drawer...'

'Your father wanted to spell...'

'I'm afraid, Jayme, dear love, that you'll have to accept that he will not take his role as your father-by-marriage lightly.'

'Oh, dearest Nerone,' she cried, loving the sound of that 'father-by-marriage', 'I'm so glad that because I wanted to picture you in every room, I started to mentally photograph the rooms in your villa before I left. I didn't get much further than your study, though.'

It was sheer bliss to be caught up in Nerone's arms again, when he had to kiss her once more. 'As I was saying,' he murmured, 'or as I think I was saying,' he teased as, holding her close to him, he returned to their conversation, 'everything was starting to peak in me so that I could not have withstood much more without taking some action. When I left you this morning—as leave I had to, or make you mine—I knew that, even though you were trying to convey verbally that you could not bear the sight of me, you must feel *something* for me. I came back to the villa intending to find out how large or small that ''something'' was, and went almost demented to discover that you and your clothes were gone.'

'You knew I'd stop off here?'

'I didn't,' he replied. 'But since it seemed a favourite place of yours, it seemed worth a ten-second stop to check.'

'We've been here a little longer than that,' she smiled lovingly, and was suddenly, tenderly brought to her feet.

'We had better go, my dear love,' Nerone smiled down into her upturned trusting face.

'Back to the villa?' she queried.

'Only for *my* passport,' he smiled. 'Luckily, since I never know when I'm likely to have to fly abroad, I've a habit of having it to hand wherever I happen to be.'

'You're—flying abroad?' queried Jayme, trying as best she could to hide how much she hated the idea of maybe not seeing him for days, or even weeks. She then learned that Nerone would never have countenanced such an idea anyway.

'After what I've been through, I'm not letting you out of my sight so soon,' he told her firmly, then delighted her totally, when he added, '*We're* flying abroad, *cara*. Though only as far as England.'

'We're going to England!' she exclaimed.

'I'm only human, beautiful Jayme,' he smiled into her startled face. 'I think we'd better leave the villa and go and confess to your mother the "true version" of what has been happening since you arrived in Italy.'

'Nerone!' she cried joyously.

'And,' he went on, 'at the same time, we can arrange for your two young sisters to be bridesmaids at the earliest possible date.'

'Oh, darling,' she breathed ecstatically. 'But we'll return to the villa some time?'

'Haven't I promised you a ride in a gondola?' he responded, and, holding her in the strong circle of his arms, he looked adoringly down into her enrapt face.

From *New York Times* Bestselling author
Penny Jordan, a compelling novel of ruthless passion
that will mesmerize readers everywhere!

Penny Jordan

Silver

Real power, true power came from
Rothwell. And Charles vowed to have it,
the earldom and all that went with it.

Silver vowed to destroy Charles, just as surely and
uncaringly as he had destroyed her father; just as he had
intended to destroy her. She needed him to want her . . .
to desire her . . . until he'd do anything to have her.

But first she needed a tutor: a man who wanted no one.
He would help her bait the trap.

**Played out on a glittering international stage,
Silver's story leads her from the luxurious comfort of
British aristocracy into the depths of adventure,
passion and danger.**

AVAILABLE IN OCTOBER!

 HARLEQUIN

You'll flip . . . your pages won't!
Read paperbacks *hands-free* with

Book Mate • I

The perfect "mate" for all your romance paperbacks

Traveling • Vacationing • At Work • In Bed • Studying • Cooking • Eating

Perfect size for all standard paperbacks, this wonderful invention makes reading a pure pleasure! Ingenious design holds paperback books OPEN and FLAT so even wind can't ruffle pages— leaves your hands free to do other things. Reinforced, wipe-clean vinyl-covered holder flexes to let you turn pages without undoing the strap . . . supports paperbacks so well, they have the strength of hardcovers!

Pages turn WITHOUT opening the strap

SEE-THROUGH STRAP

Reinforced back stays flat

Built in bookmark

BOOK MARK

BACK COVER HOLDING STRIP

10 x 7¼ opened
Snaps closed for easy carrying, too

Available now. Send your name, address, and zip code, along with a check or money order for just $5.95 + .75¢ for postage & handling (for a total of $6.70) payable to Reader Service to:

Reader Service
Bookmate Offer
901 Fuhrmann Blvd.
P.O. Box 1396
Buffalo, N.Y. 14269-1396

Offer not available in Canada
*New York and Iowa residents add appropriate sales tax.

BM-G